Prais

how to make yc

"*How to Make Your Mother Cry* is an incredible cross-cultural manifesto of word and body: What is home. What is mother. What is family. What is self. What is woman, and how do we story her."

—Lidia Yuknavitch, author of *Thrust* and *Verge*

"Urgent, intense, and intimate, the stories in Sejal Shah's *How to Make Your Mother Cry* conjure memories and stir the soul. A clever and beautifully crafted collection!"

—Deesha Philyaw, author of *The Secret Lives of Church Ladies*

"Sejal Shah has written a stunning hybrid work, and I'm in awe of its candor, risk, and craft—this is a book I will recommend to other writers, professors of creative writing, and readers of literary texts. I see Shah's book as broadening and supporting the larger conversation of work by writers of color."

—Jon Pineda, author of *Let's No One Get Hurt*

"Each sentence is its own jewel box of pleasures and delights. . . . Like works by Sara Ahmed, Audre Lorde, and Claudia Rankine, this groundbreaking collection will be a touchpoint for years and decades to come."

—Rahul Mehta, author of *No Other World*
and *Feeding the Ghosts*

"If a queer text is an unsettled one, crossing cultures, crossing genres, then this book rescripts what we think we know. Shah is a master storyteller who keeps us knowing differently. *How to Make Your Mother Cry* is bold and brave. A collection for a new century."

—Dawn Lundy Martin, author of *Good Stock Strange Blood*

HOW TO MAKE YOUR MOTHER CRY

fictions

SEJAL SHAH

west virginia university press • morgantown

First epigraph from "An Interview: Audre Lorde and
Adrienne Rich," in *Sister Outsider: Essays and Speeches*
(Berkeley: Crossing Press, 2007). Copyright © 1984, 2007
by Audre Lorde.

This is a work of fiction. Names, characters, places, and incidents
are products of the author's imagination or are used fictitiously.

ISBN 978-1-959000-13-6 (paperback) /
978-1-959000-14-3 (e-book)

Library of Congress Cataloging-in-Publication Data
Names: Shah, Sejal, 1972 –author.
Title: How to make your mother cry : fictions / Sejal Shah.
Other titles: How to make your mother cry (Compilation)

Description: First edition. | Morgantown : West Virginia University Press, 2024.

Identifiers: LCCN 2023043229 | ISBN 9781959000136 (paperback)
| ISBN 9781959000143 (ebook)

Subjects: LCGFT: Linked stories.
Classification: LCC PS3619.H3483 H69 2024
| DDC 813/.6 —dc23/eng/20231031

LC record available at https://lccn.loc.gov/2023043229

Book and cover design by Than Saffel / WVU Press
Cover image courtesy of the George Eastman Museum

To Val, Jim, Zoe, KK, and Urvashi, in memory

Valerie Jean Boyd (1963–2022)

James Wright Foley (1973–2014)

Rana Zoe Mungin (1989–2020)

Kirit Nathalal Shah (1940–2021)

Urvashi Vaid (1958–2022)

People will never tell you what you're supposed to know. You have to get it for yourself, whatever it is that you need in order to survive.

—Audre Lorde

What breaks the pattern is always very true.

—Gabrielle Civil

contents

soundtrack

"Running Up That Hill (A Deal with God)" ...... Kate Bush
"All I Have to Do Is Dream" .... The Everly Brothers
"When Doves Cry" .... Prince
"Left of Center" .... Suzanne Vega
"Blue Monday" .... New Order
"Cruel Summer" .... Bananarama
"Message in a Bottle" .... The Police
"Interlude" .... india.arie
"First Try" .... Tracy Chapman
"Spring Street" .... Dar Williams
"Fantasy" .... Earth, Wind & Fire
"Temperamental" .... Everything but the Girl
"Walking with a Ghost" .... Tegan and Sara
"Hanuman Chalisa" .... Morari Bapu
"Peace" .... Paul Kelly

I.

a girl walks into
the forest

the girl with two brothers

When I was twelve or thirteen, we lived in the house on Old Massapoag Road, and I used to dream what I thought all girls dreamt: someone snatched me, began to work off my clothes. You were there watching. Your gray eyes troubled your face. You rescued me. You pushed him and his ski mask aside. You yelled out various ways you would punish him. He ran through a side street, scaled a fence, disappeared. You stroked my face (how soft, you murmured). You kissed me. *How marvelous*, I thought. *How miraculous!* I'm breathing and I'm kissing at the same time. We ran, then walked past the high school, our blue sneakers breaking the dark. You saved the only thing worth saving. This is how our story always began.

My dreams stopped when I thought of wanting a camera—of needing some way to record. I wasn't thinking about shutter speed, about aperture, about flash.

My oldest brother was tired of my asking to borrow his things. Or of my borrowing them without asking. Before the idea of a camera, I thought of the usual things. Living in olden times, a secret conversation in a secret language (I was the only one who understood). I thought of running away, of what I would save in my house in case of fire, which albums I would grab, and which dolls.

I was all about orphanhood, the plane from Chicago crashing—we would have to go live in California with my father's brothers—one of them was our legal guardian—and I wonder who thought to tell me that—is that what parents are supposed to tell, or did I ask them, knowing how these things go, knowing how these things may go? I was always asking: *Who will take care of me if you go? How will I live if you go?*

Did all children dream these things then, in quilts of birds and falls and forgotten red bicycles? I thought of how my parents would cry uncontrollably when I died at a young age from a devastating disease. I imagined the wake, their friends circling them, the plates of slightly stale cake, the enlarged photos of me wreathing the walls, the scrapbook with every Mother's Day and birthday card I had ever made, the slightly discolored green construction paper, school glue still shining in smudges. My older brothers would cry (I had almost never seen them cry), but they would have to force the tears—I was dead after all! For once, the applause I had been waiting my whole life for.

Or: if our parents died, perished in a plane crash, would we refuse to be shipped off to California? Would we live in an abandoned train car, next to the elementary school, in the bramble near where the middle school kids came to smoke and flick their red and yellow lighters? Would we flee to New Jersey, to our other uncle's house, refusing to leave the East Coast? Where would we play our secret game: the White Witch, the Purple Policeman, the Green Ghost, circling? My oldest brother had the banana-seat bike we both wanted. My middle brother had Matchbox cars he raced for hours. All I had was Lite-Brite and makeup head Barbie.

Perhaps our relatives wouldn't want all three of us—we would have to fight to be together—we would not let ourselves be split up. Or: we'd have to fight to get to California, all three of us, crossing the Mississippi—like two cats and a dog, or two dogs and a cat. (In every scenario, I was a cat.)

I was a well-read child of all the usual fairy tales—I knew how it went. The parents never lasted beyond the first page. Some of the best ones had the parents dead before the book even began. Or the father was mean. Or the mother was crazy. Or the father was weak. Or the mother was dead. All you had was your brother, and in my case, I had two. All you ever had was your brother, and all the ways in which you hoped that he would—that any boy might—try to see you, recognize you, save you, because you were a girl, and you were worth saving. You were worth something.

*

We lived on Old Massapoag Road; it meant great waters in a language no one I knew spoke. When I wasn't searching the ground for arrowheads or a perfectly smooth pebble, I had the regular battery of fantasies: death wishes for various family members. Imagining the grief, the unbearability of it all was one way to love them. So I wanted more than a regular camera (I was an unusual child, or perhaps very ordinary). I wanted an instrument to record people I had thought about or had seen. I wanted to be able to show others something that existed only in my head. I wanted to be able to remember. I was young enough not to realize that it is better just to let things go. A story is just another way to let things go.

This is one way to tell the story: You and me and the girl on Chestnut Street. Here is another: I wanted you to save me. You wanted me to save you. Did you understand that was what we were really saying? Why not choose me? The mental refrain of gym class, of sweat, of fourth grade come back to haunt.

Older Brother One says: We'll kick his ass.

Older Brother Two says: *What* is that music you're listening to?

More books would have kept me out of trouble, but I welcomed her, trouble: running at night next to the horse farm, beer and fish tacos across the middle of the day, crouching by the guard rail, fiddle music on high; driving down 91, through Connecticut. We were on our way to New York, so there was no way to avoid Connecticut. I had always disliked Connecticut—connect and cut—telling you both things at once, not unlike a boy. When I was younger, maybe six or seven, I knew that states were male or female. Connecticut was clearly a boy. Vermont: a girl. New Hampshire is a boy: "Live Free or Die." What girl do you know who would say that? We might say it, but we don't believe it. I don't believe it.

I always said more than a single girl should: dropping the names of old boyfriends, stupid words collecting in the corners of my mouth. These are all different ways to say: You are the absence that lingers.

Older Brother One says: Remember my friend Pete, the mathematician? He's a nice guy.

You said you would soon know all my stories. As in a fairy tale, every week, I felt I had to give you a reason to leave, manufacture a reason for you to stay. You pointed out that you were turning into one of my stories. Even if this story is about you (and you knew there would be one) how do you know what I will squander to make the story better, and what I will keep, afraid?

I looked you up in the dictionary. I found you under save. There were many definitions and every one of them fit. Everything was about avoidance. The prevention of fatigue. As in: *to save one's longing*. This is what the dictionary said: *To anticipate one's desire and so to prevent. To save one's own hide or skin. To reserve or lay aside. To keep from harm.*

Older Brother Two says: I think you'd like him. He works for Intel. He knows how to ice skate.

This, then, is the frame; this, without a lens. I decided to take fewer classes. I still had to teach. Shoving back folders and files, I instructed you in sun salutations in the living room, still in my work clothes—blouse, skirt, nylons. I watched you watch me, the candy-colored stripe of underwear when my shirt lifted away; we stripped in kitchen-blind sunlight after downward dog, after upward dog. We laughed through plank. Your mouth, disarming the buttons of my skirt. The sunlight, splitting us. Your nails, ruining my nylons. Track one on repeat, track nine on repeat, beer spilling onto the kitchen floor, beer spilling from your hand, your hand knocking everything over.

We walked to the pond they call a lake and sat listening to the birds (loons? swans?). Something large from Canada. I wanted to believe they were a sign. Birds herald something in every book I ever read, and we all know how much books can help us in this world, can save us in this world.

Brother Number One calls me Chris, as in Evert Lloyd. Older Brother Two calls me Bjorn. They ascertained, together, that I hated those names. We watched tennis growing up.

I learned to take photos on a point-and-shoot. I learned only recently about light meters, about middle gray.

The inanimate objects are speaking: the damp towel darkening the back of the door. The coffee pot, empty, but still on. I walk outside to toss papers in the recycling bin. It is difficult to return to the quiet of where I live.

Older Brother One calls, but I don't pick up. He reminds me not to miss Brother Two's birthday. He leaves the mathematician's number on the machine. No pressure, he says.

There is no surface I did not wash or vacuum when you left. Let me be clear here. Everything has been picked up, held, and replaced. It's not that everything was bad. I had been craving something. What you gave me was something. It felt, at the time, like something.

Chrissy, my brothers say: You should have more than just something.

When I was younger, I didn't know the language that contained Massapoag. (Now I know: Algonquin.) Back then, I looked where I always looked: the dictionary, world books, the encyclopedia. Who is Indian? Who does the word belong to?

Twenty years ago, books were school, mirror, portal: it was the only way to search or travel. I found this definition: *any of the hunted players in the children's game of cowboys and Indians*. But books are wrong, too: faulty maps drawn by people who want to set something straight. But it was never straight; it was crooked, shady. *West Indian, East Indian, American Indian*: all people named by people who were not Indian at all.

In the dictionary, there was also India ink, Indian path, Indian meal, and Indian yellow. The last was something my second brother would like*: an orange-yellow pigment obtained from the urine of cows fed on mango leaves*. It would make him laugh. Think of mangoes. We are this kind of Indian, by which I mean East, but no one I know actually uses the term. *East Indian.* Who are these words for? *We know.* No one from these places.

I don't want you, now, to know anything real about me, but you know this: I hated to get off the phone with you. You said you knew I would immediately dial another number: Brother One or Two or my mother. Anything to fill the space. Learn to live with it, you said. You are stronger, you said. You were leaving again for Chestnut Street.

She is the girl who frames photos of your sisters and your mother. She can group them on your bureau (the one you painted together) and three-two-one, one-two-three, one-three-two their order. She arranges your life. She can take photographs, fresh from the camera, from the night chemicals, and magnet them to the fridge, pin them to cork, leave them on the dashboard until they curl like canoes. These are the photos that belong. You record all the major holidays of the year. I always thought of her as your weekend. (I believed that I counted in your real life.) This is what I most regret.

I won't pick up my address book. I never called you back. I'm learning to play my CDs all the way through. It bothered you that I played so many songs on repeat.

For the first ten weeks after you left, I could sense times of day or night when you might also have been thinking of me. I could feel it—I was sure of this once or twice. But I can no longer feel what you are thinking. What might end up on a list you will make.

Whether you ever even told her. What you tell yourself: I have no idea.

Brother Two says: Of course, he didn't tell her. Why would he tell her? He doesn't want to end up alone. Didn't we teach you anything? Never trust a guy.

But neither of my brothers ever met you, ever saw how you looked at the lake, ever heard how you pronounced Mass-a-po-ag, how you listened to my stories. Still: you have turned into what we always suspected—a ghost in a string of ghosts. A ghost with mediocre teeth and a good heart. A ghost with a weakness for girls with bright eyes and blurred edges. Predictable: a weakness for weak girls.

Maybe you have no need of a magic camera, of a way to record. How do you order your memory? How do you make your garden grow?

Maybe you think only of the girl on Chestnut Street. When you die, though, I will be a mourner at your wake.

I think you would also come to my wake, partake in the cake, the yellow cake separating from frosting, the way I hear skin will pull away from bone. You will fork mouthfuls just to do something.

You will look at the blown-up photos, my unusually large teeth. You would look at the row of dolls I made of clothespins, acorns, and quilt scraps. You would see the family of Indians sitting to the side. You would say you were my friend. I would nudge the pink into your neck until finally you left for a cigarette and a magazine, a cigarette and a drive, a cigarette and a drink. You would shake my older brothers' hands. You would stand with my family, looking at my picture, and then this is the picture that would help me go, release me from this spinning. By this time, when I am in the ground, only my molars will last, the metal fillings outlasting all skin; my hair and nails still growing, unable to stop.

This is a story about what will never happen. This is a story about things that never happened. Watch me annihilate you. There was no great fire, no plane crash. There was no wake, no crossing of rivers. We walk toward a mountain. We long for the curve in the road. We look at each other, heads leaning in. You are carrying a staff. The girl's face is happy. I could never see your face.

*

You were a book I misread. Perhaps you were the assailant (tall white male, half-day's growth, abused by your father, angry at the world), but I couldn't recognize you without the ski mask. I wanted you to be the one watching out for me. I didn't want to see what all the wise men and wiser women gently warned me about: You were one of many to keep watch for. What is it that the wise ones say: *Keep walking and you will avoid so much of this, you will find your way. You can walk away.* The elders are patient and they smile at me. The old ones raise their hands, a simultaneous greeting and farewell. Yes, I answer them. I will walk in well-lit areas. I will not walk alone.

I am the maiden, the lookout, the sentry. I am the only doll I must save in case of fire. I will stop-drop-and-roll. I will join my brothers outside. They will bridge their arms to steady me, they will finally get along. I will not be alone.

Even on the phone with my brothers, I start to hum, then sing. The CD wants to play the song all the way through, but why should any track end? All I have to do is dream. Dream, dream. I can't stop myself from reaching back to press play again: from wanting the song to stay in that moment, that perfect pitch of longing.

Older Brother Two: Would you stop with the crappy music already?

When you are on Chestnut Street, or Avocado, or Citrus—or any of those fucking fruit streets—your eyes will mark the photo of the two of you on Fire Island from last summer or the summer before. Perhaps you will walk over to the bureau and pick up the photo, lightly tap the edges so that the picture is not crooked in the frame, so that it lies flat and it lies straight. You will hold it in your hands and then place it back on the dresser, not exactly over the dustless spot. I know you well enough to know that while you notice too much, you will not notice that.

This is the picture, which is framed. This is how I must think of you. Photos of us are spooled away, unexposed—I catch sight of them and their weak teeth at the edge of sleep. They smudge the edges of mirrors with their persistence, with their terrible vision of another way, with their unreasonable longing. And what state would that be? It's a photo, overexposed—too much sunlight blinding us. After what is left pushes at us, beginning.

This is not the only story of what happened between us, but it is the only one I will tell.

What is the point of telling you that I still wake up remembering (as though you are here!) your childhood-blue eyes. How you used to look at me. As though you were waiting to hear whatever story might begin. *No one saves anyone.* As though you wanted to sit on my floor, tipping back bottles, draining bottles, collecting words, and looking at me, for a very long time. As though you were more than unreliable teeth and heart. Your eyes, a kind of frame. My hands, enough. As though you had decided to stay.

Even now I hear my older brothers talking. *Hasn't she been listening to us? Move on, Chrissy. Stop perseverating.* And I want to tell them, I was listening all the time. I was watching you all the time. What girls are tossing their sheets, dreaming of your backs, thinking you will turn around, that you are not merely gathering your jackets and your wallets, that you are not merely preparing to walk away? You are just boys, walking. You were just a boy, walking. No one saves anyone.

letter i never sent

Dear Mr. Bird,

    Here I am at my arangetram. Are you away in the summer? Did you finish your dissertation? I liked it when you played the guitar for us that one day. Is it OK to write to you? Are you going to move back to North Carolina?

                    Your student, V.

mary, staring at me

Angela was the oldest person I have met who was my age. Maybe you knew someone in your younger life who was beautiful. Do you remember your fascination with the pink of her face, with the books that lined her bookcase, with the doll bought in France, with those flat stacks of records? Did this girl have an antique dresser with a lock? And did she string the key on a ribbon? Was it a white silk ribbon—was it a slender key?

Remember where your parents shopped. Your mother twisted your hair and your sister's into two plaits, so you wouldn't forget where you came from. You had no words to tell her (you could never tell her) that seventh graders don't let anyone forget. She sent you to school in imitation Zips. Your metal lunch box banged against your hip as you ran to catch the bus. Your hair slapped the air behind you, too tightly braided to sail the way white hair sails.

If this girl was black (that's what we said then, black),

she lived on Canterbury Road. Maybe she had a side garden lined with pink and white peonies, and an adopted brother named Sam. Maybe you co-wrote a report on crustaceans and coelenterates. You both knew it was only a matter of time before she was drafted by the black table, and you were sent to the freaks. Sometimes, you met in the middle of the lunchroom to laugh over lunch ladies, tater tots, and gossip.

Her parents could have come from China and you would have wanted slippers that folded into thinness and a calendar that followed the moon. You wanted whatever it took to get the antique dresser and the doll from France. Every girl wants a white ribbon pulled straight by the weight of a key. A ribbon for your hair, a key that doesn't have to open anything.

I want to tell you about Angela.

We stole food, and we stole dance classes. I met her in class, at Pamela Pointer's studio, Our Lady of Lourdes, lower level. We arrived early to change from our street clothes, to prepare. We stepped into the immediate coolness that basements and churches have. We tied our hair back. We soaked our mouths with sections of ripped grapefruit and stepped onto the black floor to stretch.

We stretched, tugging our ankles and the loose elastic

ends of our leotards, citrus fiber caught beneath our nails, poor French manicures. All around us, other girls, but we never talked until class was over. *Demi-pliés, tendus, port de bras, jetés.*

Our Lady of Lourdes smelled of dust, of Ben-Gay, of the faint remainder of incense, of prayer. We turned on our sides and swung our legs like metronomes, but more heavily weighted, so that there was a pause, a breath at the top of the motion. We prayed through the first stretches, runner's stretches, knees at ninety-degree angles followed by abdominal crunches. Our legs in ripped tights: fuchsia, black, navy, jade. *Chassé, pas de bourrée; glissade! Glissade!*

Sometimes we checked our names off without stuffing money into the envelope. Bill never said anything, but he had a way of looking at you. Even though he was slow in the head, Bill, he could look at you. I never talked about it with Angela. I pressed my cheek against the cold concrete pillar until the red lifted from my face. I found my smudged fingers pressing into piles of discarded prayer books. Cracked maroon leather. Hymnals spilled out of stacks of breaking boxes under single moon-colored bulbs, frayed strings fluttering. Here a tarnished mirror, a rotting section of bench. A costume rack of choir robes, unhooked. Everything exhales prayer. Everything begs to be remembered.

Some days we had money to buy smoothies after class. Some nights we went to her apartment for tea. Angela was between boys, ignoring the ones who flocked to her. They were insects to a light, lacking imagination. I don't think I would have ignored them—maybe because I never learned how. We drank fruit: kiwi, bananas, passion fruit, strawberries—Angela and me.

Everyone wants a key that opens nothing.

Angela lives alone and moves when the rent climbs over her waitressing tips and secondhand ingenuity. Men fall over themselves to dance with her at W———'s, where we go nearly every Friday night. They come to her, their tiny wings thrashing. She sits at the bar, smokes her cigarettes, looks past them. Some nights I am there with her, watching them falter, taking note—the white boys in the punk bands; the suburban sleepy-eyed black boys; the university boys exhaling their uniform scent of wool, cash, and cigarettes—jangling their keys like a threat. I met Alan when I was sitting with Angela. Sometimes I wonder if he wasn't really coming over to talk to her. Isn't everyone always hedging their bets?

Angela says: I don't think you knew me, or you wouldn't say that.

There was always the boy she slept with and the one she

talked to on the phone before she slept. These were usually different boys. We lent each other black sweaters and biographies. I find my books smoothed into her shelves, tucked in alphabetically as though they had always belonged there. Sometimes I do not find them at all.

We go to the fabric store to buy material for curtains. We hover above the remainder bin: we search through tight scrolls of cloth, sealed like medieval missives. Blood-red corduroys, the fingered weave of British-blue damask, its reversible ever-widening ovals. Some we lifted and some we paid for. That day we both had money, and Angela wanted curtains. She wants the world at rest when she sleeps. We left carrying bundles of cream-colored linen raised every few inches in an exclamation, a knot of thread. The mistake, they say, is woven into Persian rugs. Every culture rationalizes the skipped note, the broken thread; every culture wants a seamless history. There is no seamless history.

I used to drive Angela home after dance class. Sometimes she'd ask me to come in. I have to go, I'd tell her. Alan was waiting. She'd say, *Come on.* It was dark in my car, but she was rolling her eyes; I could always hear it in her voice. Other times, she would sing-song a message into my answering machine: We're going to get grits and coffee—I'll be there in twenty minutes. Are you there, V_____?

I don't like her—that's all that Alan ever had to say. Most nights he works on his dissertation and drinks. Single malt whiskey or dark (expensive) beer, but only after dinner. Jim Beam if he hasn't been paid. I thought he was smart, and that maybe it would rub off on me. On Fridays, the days I don't work, I look through his bookshelves. He has them in some kind of special order. He could always tell if I had taken one out. Lots of criticism, the A–Z of Hollywood cinema, the seminal autobiographies of ethnicity. I joked that he collected women like paint samples, but what was I supposed to say? I was younger and not very sharp about men. He never forced me to sleep with him, but he used to say that sex put him in a better mood.

Angela pours cured sesame oil on me, and it slips toward my lowest back, to the bones that form a bowl, to the bones that argue beneath the skin.

Take your shirt off, she tells me and I don't want to go home. We were in her kitchen, and I was sitting on a stool. *Go lie down in there*, she orders. *I'm going to warm this up*. She disappears, and I hear the faint metallic chirping of her microwave.

Angela had money that night, and we blew it at the juice bar and a carafe of bitter red wine after class. Carafe. The word stayed in my mouth after the wine, while I rocked back and forth on the battered wooden stool in Angela's kitchen, listening to the whir-and-click of her cooking.

I was named after a river in India, and I have never been there. My real name means quiet. Alan says talk, and I do. He says I talk and talk (and I do). But my real name is still Quiet. I should never have had to explain this to you.

Angela and I are almost the same color. She will not check off any boxes on any forms. She will not let them place her in one tribe or the other. Once she asked Alan just what exactly cultural studies *is*. I tried not to laugh. She stared at him as though he were a Russian ghost. Her arms cut through air, curved blades. You might think that I put her on a pedestal. Alan says that. You don't have to have a PhD to know that he is jealous.

Angela says: I want to go to Africa. I want to go somewhere. I want to get out of this city, this country. How can you stay?

Someone has to stay.

Her hands are gorgeous, a pair of strangely aristocratic cyclamen. When they press against my back, I lean. I lean into her and begin to talk. My back twists into the treble clef. Her fingers court the dissonant tendon. I see

Angela's clogs, kicked into the corner, and they disturb the dust.

When I taught school, the kids said dance, and I said no. Later, Angela said dance, and I sat on top of my hands and blew exaggerated breaths to cool my tea. She said please, and I said OK, push the chairs back and be quiet. You have to not laugh. I pulled flowers and flutes from my arms. My arms grew branches and poked through the ceiling of the Mission. Mary at our table, sunken into plaster and surrounded by colored glass, her gown falling and fixed, that Mary, she stared. She watched me whirling in the narrow aisle between two rows of tables. I waited for snowflakes to cover the stage between us. We were falling and fixed, drinking fruit: crushed ice, orange juice, overripe bananas.

Oh, Angela! Dark heart darkening the bitter water. Your hand cresting across my hip, nipples breaking the water, a pair of lilies, rising. Is that really what I would say? Seaweed, sluicing the lower columns like hair. Water salting beneath my ears; a hand notched into the small of my back. The blue escaping me. It was the postage stamp of blue fixed in your bathroom, Angela. You framed Guatemala, and it stared back at me from the quiet of your eyes. Blue covering me, legs flail but nothing hidden and my bones embarrass me. You hold me and you wash me. Your lips unnerve my neck.

I open my mouth, the bitter smell of crushed almonds. Alan calls and we listen to his voice leaving a message on the machine. *You smooth my cotton shirt across my navel. The color, you tell me, is beautiful.*

*

Once, at the Y, Angela and I ran through the machines— hulks of metal and steel, moving our limbs in slow motion, as if underwater. We shucked our clothes and sprinted, tiny steps, into the showers. We gazed at each other, glorious, wet. Three heads spraying water into a garden of tile. We were children! We were girls! She hugged me. We fold our arms around each other and held on, under the water. My heart rattles beneath its thin stem of sternum. We laugh at my hair, skulled around my head like a cap, and hers spiraling outward, the lopsided spires of a child-drawn sun.

Angela: I think it is pity I saw in your eyes. It was a miniature doll I saw, collapsing on the table. She appears disturbed, her French features even tighter, her ivory dress starched, as though in terror. Her eyes are dumb blue planets. Mary, where were you? The smell of liniment, the fortitude. Three colored stones to grant me sight. The body is the first to go. Baubles, wafer, communion, host. I can read Angela's eyes and *we will not kiss like this again.*

I stop on my way home, everything rising to points. Inside, sunshine, pooled in corners. A pile of postcards from the West—New Mexico, Arizona, Utah. The weight of the doors tempts me. Mary suffers inscrutably from the corner. What if I climbed to the top? What would I find there? Her son wears his hair loose and his hand lifted—in greeting? In farewell? I sit until my back aches, and real churchgoers appear. *They will know I don't know how long to stay and when to leave.*

Alan is talking when I walk up the stairs. I will start the water for a bath. Right knob turned all the way, left knob turned a little. I want to find something. I want to add something to the water and turn it blue. Something that will hide the shallowness of the tub, something to make the water bearable.

The tap is still running. Bright red commas, semi-colons, Spanish stigmata. I will sit in the water, look at the ceiling as though it were a mirror. I will examine my body for marks and inventions. I will shave my legs until blood appears. I am waiting for a sign.

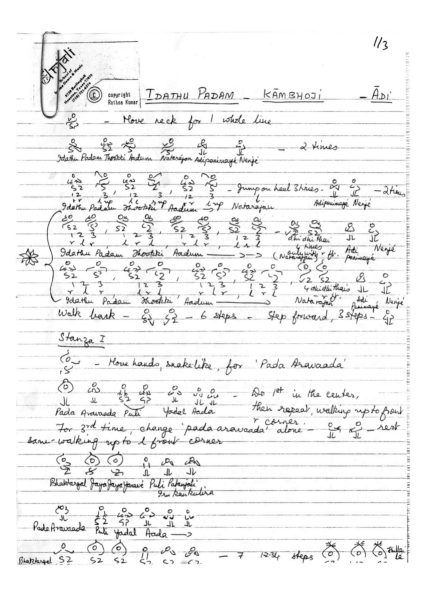

letter i never sent

Hi Mr. Bird,

    I like a boy who was in your class. Don't guess who. Do you know Beth Teegarden? Did you see me at Halloween? I am taking gymnastics lessons. Could you tell I was supposed to be a princess? I am only good at the floor. I think it is nice that your wife is Chinese. We wore tall hats like princesses.

        Yours,

        V.Z.K.

dicot, monocot

Do you remember the sixth grade, Margaret? Blood and
Foreign Language beginning the same year. There was
that line between all the girls then. An extra bone, a hor-
izontal spine—. A keloid inch scripted onto my chest, a
fossil, an unreadable note, the first of all the unanswerable signs.

We counted. We all counted. You know what I mean.
Even if we didn't talk about it all the time, you remember. Even if we never talked about it, you know what I
mean.

Maybe you should have kept it, our book. I still have it.
You would have tossed it—maybe by the seventh grade.
I still have it, our book. What do you remember? Re-
member, remember. As if I could hold us at twelve.

Miss Merrill had all of us, every science class in the sixth
grade. Remember that day when all the boys had to
leave the room? (No one could hold us at twelve.) I don't
think they ever told us where they went. Miss Merrill

had the bluest eyes. Did you ever wonder if they were real? It was a long time ago. Did Nick ever tell you I saw him with no underwear? We were out back by the creek.

I still have the book. I know Nick probably threw his out. Maybe your mom made him. You don't take stuff like that to California. *Toothed monocot.* Do you know that the weeping willow is a toothed monocot? We knew this once. We had a page for the silver plants. We snuck into the Jones's backyard, but I was afraid of Daisy.

Dusty Miller: *lobed dicot.* Lamb's Ear: smooth. We didn't know then: The silver rubs off—. The conifers are the next page. Pitch smeared under the plastic covering. We draw pictures of the leaves next to the leaves themselves. You will not remember this. We are only eleven. No one counted at eleven. Did I ever tell you about your brother? It was a long time ago.

You moved to California, Margaret (how could you?). You didn't even take our book. I still have the gingko we found at the end of my street (*Monocot lobed*). A Japanese tree splitting itself into two—mitosis, mitosis—leaves like fans; pleated. We thought they were special, but there were whole trees of them. The tulip tree was one street over (*Dicot lobed toothed*). By the end of November, we could have found our way there by counting rows of bark, the first language beneath our hands.

Do you remember the most special one? The one we went into Elm Lane for? We weren't allowed, and we went anyway. (No one could hold us at twelve—.) We found a tree that had leaves like stars. Sweet gum; we looked it up in the book (there must have been a book). *(Dicot lobed toothed.)*

I didn't put on anything special to save them. We were only ten or eleven. What did we know about fixatives? I think we glued them to the paper. We probably used school glue. We had to use my mother's sewing needles to open the bottle; you know how it always stops up.

It had been so long when we stopped hearing from you. We never found out who spray-painted "Ozzy Lives" near the creek. You were going to be a ballerina. *Crimean linden, Verbanica magnolia, white oak, pussy willow.* What did you become when you grew up? *Saucer magnolia. Star magnolia.* No one could hold us at twelve.

Did Nick ever tell you he saw me without underwear that one time? We had a page for the silver plants. It was out back by the creek. And did you become a dancer? A weeping willow is a toothed monocot. Or did your bones get bigger? It's OK if your bones got bigger. You know you can't help it, your bones.

I want to believe that this is a confession,
a powerful longing for the first time of
change-sexuality blooms.   There was that
    line between girls, keloid itch - scar continually
(unanswerable) re-opened and re sewn — there is a division of
    dicots, monocots.
    -Boys have to separate, leave room - they go to
    their sex ed training, books the mapping of
    intimate, details, the mapping of differences,
    the collecting of insides, of fluids, of flowering
    parts.
    - mitosis, girl's dress parting - every girl wanted
    more than one.
    - special experience at Elm street, finding the
    star shaped star, sweet gum — the thing
        that was to shape her ⇒ but to Margret
        What did you become? Star Magnolia or
                            Saucer Magnolia

    -You know you can't help it, who you are,
        your bones ⇒ return to idk an extra
        bone, chromosone, difference in nature

    Really nice, a thrilling read.
                            Jim

letter i never sent

Dear Mr. Bird,

My brother says I should go ahead in Math. Track starts today. One time you banged my desk down, you were so mad. I look up words I do not know. I think you look nice in glasses. It is almost August now. Dissertation. Mandarin.

Yours,

mandala

As a child, I heard the highway and knew it was the ocean, knew that it was the sound of water lapping, then rushing. Never mind that the closest water is a lake that breeds zebra mussels, floating fish, more snow. We lived in a city rusted out on the shores of a Great Lake. We almost never even saw the lake. Snow blanking our rememberings nine months of the year, no swimming allowed the other three. One summer, I remember just walking back and forth on the boardwalk, the pier, all of us, passing by those boys walking and nudging each other. And Lata stopped and held out her hands. As if to mimic the shoreline, as if to hold back the water. The lighthouse light passed her and then swept back, and I saw her the way I see her still: broken glass, beach-ground glass, smooth, worn. Still.

*

Children will not believe they are landlocked. Cassava, jamfur, mogro, mango. Canada was a story our parents told us. Gerrard Street, Patel Brothers grocery stores;

Toronto was an endless street of saris, spices, dried goods we couldn't get over here. Canada was a choice of restaurants, a fast-food place for chaat, chaa, burfi. I remember corn on the grill, sold outside, on the street, with salt and chili-lime; roasted—the way our parents made on summer picnics.

Our mother prayed for another daughter (this was unusual). Once in a generation, violet eyes. Lata, when she was angry, used to say that she had never been asked. She had been called. My mother called for her, and obedient, the moon followed the sun. The moon swallowed the earth. Once in a generation, unusual eyes. Our grandfather had them, has them, too.

*

We lived our lives in other girls' basements. At birthday parties, we played pin the tail on the donkey. A half-dozen basement walls of upside-down exclamation points in the wrong place. My favorite part: the blindfold, the birthday girl's mother tying the bandana, smoothing your hair out of the way, her cool hands resting on your cheek, double-knotting it behind your head, a tug to make sure it will hold, and then turning you, turning. The other girls joined in, turning you, turning, until you were spinning; dizzy. What could you see then, through the blue or red camp kerchiefs? I would shut my eyes, then. They laughed while you tried to walk. It felt like smoking later did.

At one summer party, a no-school birthday, there was an animal hanging from a tree. This Mother had taken an adult education class at the high school and learned papier-mâché. This time, they sent us out with sticks. Blindfolded, a girl hit a tree with her broomstick. She thought it was the animal; she kept hitting, waiting for the break. They told her, it's not the right place. The mother tried to grab her, but she came at them, swinging. I had the stick. When the animal exploded, hard candy flew out like rain.

*

The wind whipped our hair. We walked until there was sand between our teeth. Toronto, a mile of lights blinking beneath the fog; flat gray rocks piled like the pellets of a prehistoric beast. They spoke French on the other side. This was our shore—the only one we knew.

Lata and I knew better. We were smart. I thought we thought the same things. That we remembered the same things: nighttime raids of the cabinet above the oven where our mother always hid the chocolate. Riding our bikes without helmets over the two highway overpasses and the street with no shoulder; sneaking out for cigarettes. I thought we did all the worst things together: drinking screwdrivers that year of bat mitzvahs, looking through Shelly's uncle's old *Playboys,* hanging out by the train tracks in Pittsford where the kids from Brighton would not make it out, so many summers later.

She hadn't even finished high school. I thought it wasn't serious. I told her to just wait; things were better in college. It was one way to get away.

*

I live and work at the Zen Center now. An old villa, adobe, and a carriage house, a gate. Inside, a Japanese garden, a sudden topiary: everything waiting, everything at ease. There is a statue of a Buddha there, fashioned from rock, faceless and serene. He dwarfs me and this comforts me. I always sit a moment at the base. Then rise, brush the crabapple petals from the stone. I sweep the front walk for my seva.

The gate is latched but unlocked. Grapevines twist around each other like double-helix DNA. They extend beyond the top of the gate to pull at the joggers on the sidewalk. These vines look like girls to me, caught, changed, as in mythology. It is not the kind of neighborhood, I think, that is bothered by the narrower sidewalk. Even the Tibetan monks pause in front of the gate. The excess of grapevines causes you to change your pace, to slightly angle away before opening the latch.

Two monks are practicing tai chi in the inner garden. I can see, from where I stand, the curve of their arms suddenly jutting out and then disappearing. They move together in a kind of quiet synchronization, the almost-sorrow that characterizes any stroke of calligraphy. The almost-joy. That still choreography, a gliding on wooden floors that characterizes us in pairs, quiet heat, before the animal lunging rises up, takes over.

By the time I reach the end of the walk, my arms ache. Still, it is a task, and one that I can see the end of, even as I first pick up the broom. That is not something that came easily to me. Repeating the task, day after day. I grasp the iron railing in my hands. Rust hennas my palms in brief designs.

I used to cross the streets of Harvard Square, the trance of ecstatic dancing in Indian print skirts and peach-colored cotton dhotis. (I wondered, what did their American parents think?) Their pale, domed heads. These were the Hare Krishnas, and I often stood briefly transfixed, before moving away. I knew my attention would cause them to approach and I only wanted to watch.

This vine-entangled gate. Grapevines wind into a system of signs I can't follow and I am suddenly tired, looking at their tenacity, their lushness. The monks are practicing in the secret garden, and I am out here, thinking again.

*

Lata and I swam around each other, hovered like the inside of a Magic 8 Ball. We floated and turned and gave inscrutable answers to everyone but each other. We were the twins, LuvKush, CastorPollux, geminous. We lived in the same body once, but we did not live there at the same time.

I left New England. I returned to the city of my parents, the one I thought I would always leave, always be leaving. Lata left, and so I stayed. Lata and I never danced with our father, he wouldn't dance with his daughters, not any Gujarati father I know, not any Indian fathers I know.

At the Zen Center, I sweep the sidewalk, roll the yoga mats, punch the indentations out of the meditation pillows and stack them by the windows; I slice carrots, shell peas in exchange for a room, a cotton sheet, a window, a set of tasks. Repetition, to keep the water away. Adho Mukha Svanasana, in class, every Monday, Wednesday, sometimes Fridays.

When no one is there, I play music by a Dutch pianist. I can never remember his name. I can't understand what he is saying. It is better that way. No space between sound and the experience of sound. The Tibetans come in, and I wonder what they think of me, stacking meditation cushions, emptying out darkened matches and the stick ends of incense. Listening to Dutch piano music. I wonder if they think of me at all. They are monks, after all.

I buy a book of tickets to the foreign-language cinema in town. It is across East Avenue, a theater connected to George Eastman's house, an island in the middle of gardens. I walk through these gardens, sequined with branches of yellow star flowers, an early excess of forsythia. I remember Alan and I visited nearly all the parks around town, faces flushed, shirts untucked.

There were benches in this garden; I remembered the concrete against my back. The pressure of my back against concrete, almost to pain. The darkened room flickers with Natalie Wood's face. *Splendor in the Grass.* Everyone who is beautiful turns. She was a girl who needed to hold her head under water, until she could forget her name.

Before my sister killed herself, I would not have stood, transfixed, in front of the Hare Krishnas singing, dancing; their green eyes, magnets. I would have gone to college and stayed there. I think I would have stayed. What I mean is that I might not always be trying to remember. *Come join us, come join us*, they chanted. I don't know anything. Before my sister killed herself, I did not count the floors of parking garages, or choose to sweep the walk so carefully. No Americandancing. I would not have tried until there was nothing to lose. Till I knew how easy it is to Americandance, to Americandrink, to Americansleepover, to Americancallyoulater, to Americanforget.

Before floats around me, the color of Ba's eyes, cloudy with cataracts. Here were maps we couldn't read to places we had never seen. These things I remember: the blue of the just-dead TV. The richness of a vodka-soaked olive, the sharp vinegar taste. Carbon paper, worn-out. Let me count the ways. The color of the unswimmable lake. The mimeographed sheets from before, Miss Hauge, Ms. Devin, Miss O'Brien, Mr. Bird, reading, math, social studies, English, talks too much, easily distracted, not trying to the best of her ability. Girl that never was.

The Tibetans came from Ithaca. They stayed at the Zen Center. I brushed the sidewalk so their feet stepped cleanly. The museum commissioned them to build a public sand painting, circles and circles: a mandala. Meditate for us, they asked. We want to watch you work. Teach us your wise ancient culture. We will bring the schoolchildren and photographers. You will wear your maroon robes and smile.

With tiny metal instruments, they blew and shook and cajoled the sand, primary colors, in symmetrical designs. One monk's only responsibility was the outside perimeter of white. Sometimes I thought I saw him look up at the people watching.

After the sand painting was finished, there would be a celebration, and then the mandala, this series of circles, color lines as thin as veins, would be swept away. I wondered how they felt destroying their work. I wondered if they felt some relief.

There must have been a time when Lata and I spoke Gujarati like breathing. (We learned French. Someday, we would leave for a place like Toronto or Québec, sometime we would fly to a place like London or Paris.) I can't remember that time, now. Mari pase sapna nathi. We learned in school never to give it your best, never try as hard as you can. Kem-em? We learned: Keep some of that juice for yourself. Thak lagvanu che. It doesn't always come back. We could see it in the teachers who had turned gray. They croaked grammar back at us, outlined their cigarette-thinned mouths with too-bright lipsticks when they thought we were filling out workbook pages. We carved cryptic messages on the desks to kids in other classes.

We studied ancient Egypt in social studies. We faked our families' coats of arms. Nearly everyone had one parent from somewhere else, even if it was Yonkers, Long Island,

Manhattan, California, the Philippines. At dances, girls bent over each other, peonies. Nipple buds, small fists *Don't look at me!* We walked the perimeter of the gym in pairs or threes, and boys zigzagged like electrons around us. Electrons and boys liking you some day: more things teachers told us about that we couldn't see.

No one talked about Lata, after. No one knew what to say. I wanted to keep talking. It was a time before I could stop. No one talked about Tibet then, ever. When I sweep the walk, each brush I am breath-in, breath-out. Now I am quiet. In the unit on Egypt, I was Cleopatra, sister of the moon, kohl edging my eyes. I directed all their gazes. I am Mira, sister of the sister of the hidden asp.

When I sweep the walk, I am a chant, Lata Meena, LataMeena, Latameena. It is a way to dance, no rust-colored robes brushing the ground, no ochre markings, no rosary of polished fruit pits hitting my chest, no banging at my chest. Till the skin breaks open, creature piñata; against quiet veins of color, the blood begins to rise.

Divination

When madness lifts an arm or head, the agate aunt arrives.
Sequester to an empty room, the seamless silence, the spinning wheel.
Lock the door. Begin. Begin again. We climb the ladder of the spine
in increments. A deft response, to torque away from color till
she courts the greening sculptures, lambs risen from the dead.
Gesture illumines the cardamom breath: the scepters back
below the back, the night prophesying the night—all like you once said.
Any gaze or tilt of head pre-supposes loss, these artifacts
of a dozen leaf-less corners. Malaise means nothing to the forest
more Latinate than hours fixed in place. Begin. Begin again, begin.
I dreamt your eyes, Japanese garden, a narrow topiary of thinnest
blue. A convent, a covenant, an olive shawl to baste the rain to skin.
This is what the shoulders say: Draw the hunter against the curtain's fall,
a velvet weight. When she calls, wear winter's wisdom to the ball—or none at all.

letter i never sent

Dear Mr. Bird,

    Did you finish your book? I am not with the slow kids. This year I am going to camp. Was I supposed to say sorry that day? I remember when you played the song. Beth and I are going to make hats. I am always the last one to eat dinner. I liked it when you wrote in our journals.

                Yours truly,
                Me (hint: you said
                I talk a lot)

II.

a girl is lost in the woods

independence, iowa

In Decorah, the train station became a
    chiropractor's office
(Everything was once something else—)
We are driving up along the Mississippi because
    I did not push
to look at the map myself and you wanted to get
    lost. I mean:
now we are watching a train go by, blocks of red—
and driving on a blue bridge while the light is
    bright that way it is
before falling. The only choices are Wisconsin or
    Illinois:
to take 52 up through Dubuque, or to stop. To rest.
It's the sound of the wheels on the bridge
hollow, before I finally have a moment, of lift.

Driving back from Cedar Rapids, we pass
    cornfields: stalks dying,
stalks dried. Independence has the most
    beautiful train station—

I think the country out here is full of them. We
    passed a train station when driving.
You said: I'd like to hop trains someday. The
    world is full of things
we haven't done. Or said: In this corner of Iowa I
    feel far from everyplace else.
The most beautiful train station was once
    something else.

We stopped in a town you had once visited with
    someone else. I wanted to take you
to a restaurant that I love. One that reminds me of
    another place I once lived: the wooden bar
jewel-like lighting along tracks. Each bridge is that
    bridge, each smattering of lights, those lights
I remember, all the ways in which they sang out.
    It was Christmas every night in Brooklyn.
Just walking was a view. I live here now, that
    place Easterners insist is big sky, paper flat.

But the sky was more than big. It was everything.
    And so much of our drive
was through land that curved; that was not, and
    never had been, flat.

— Idathu Padam Jhokki Aad...

Walk back — —

Stanza I

— Move hands, snake-li...

Pada Aravaada Puli   Yodal Aa...

For 3rd time, change 'pac...

...e—walking up to l front c...

how to make your mother cry

Before you left for Baltimore, you bought me *Blue Train*, still despising the quality of my only Coltrane CD, a *Best of* compilation. What you wore: a coat that was more expensive than I could properly imagine. You told me what I needed: a subscription to *The Nation*. To go with you to the George Clinton concert.

One Friday, you finished teaching. My classmates, they trailed out the door. We went to dinner. We drank Jim Beam and careened toward each other. Jim Beam. Us: the logical extension of the first time your hand rested, a little more than briefly, on my arm. We were together for more than a year.

This was the prompt you gave to our writing class: Who knows how to make love stay? This was the question I answered instead: Who knows how to make her mother cry? I do. After you left, I did.

Remind her of how you got in trouble in the fourth

grade. How she sent you to school with the wrong word. What you needed was eraser. You don't care what the British say. How have they ever helped you? You say to her: You should know what the right word for eraser is. You should not send your daughter off to school with the word rubber and a walnut-and-cream-cheese sandwich.

I would not speak to her for that whole afternoon. We watched the end of the soaps in silence. I let her make me an afternoon snack.

Drink coffee instead of tea. This will make you American.

She's lying. She says India when someone asks where she's from—and it's not where she grew up. I want to tell you that. None of her passports have ever said anything about India. Not her birth certificate. Nothing except her marriage license, perhaps, which I've never even seen. And how about that marriage: she doesn't make a fuss, so my father doesn't bring her flowers. Whom do you dislike most now? My father, for not bringing home flowers; my mother, for not making him; me, for keeping track?

She will worry about yellowing teeth, she will worry about caffeine.

She cannot pronounce her *h*'s. On the phone, she is careful, speaking slowly, enunciating for the Americans who will ask her, What? What are you saying? How do you spell that? But your English is good: can you say that again? Flinch. Refuse to read what she writes: your gym excuses, your home-sick-from-school notes, her thank-you notes, her letters. Decide that you will be an English teacher, an English professor, that you will study it, that you will be what she is not.

This is how to make my mother cry. She has braided and oiled it, braided and washed it, braided your hair into two plaits. She wants the world to see that you are Indian the way she can see it (it is as natural to her as breathing). She wants to give you something other women will envy. She wants to give you a middle part. She tells you that coconut oil smells good, but it does not; not until the Body Shop markets it a decade later. Once something is out of England, it's OK. Once something is swallowed by England, hennaed and remixed, it's OK. Rubbers, though; that will never be OK. Beg her to cut your hair.

She tells you that your hair will be shiny, that your hair will last, that it will not fall out like hers—that you will draw everyone's envy. Hair will be your power, your secret weapon. Hair is the way to catch a man, to catch the eye of the right one.

But you cannot braid it yourself. This is a problem
at camp. You cannot wash it yourself—it is too long.
This is a problem after gym. Beg for bangs, for shoul-
der-length. The weight snaps your head back, when
your hair is wet (and straight, finally). Your arms tire.
Gordon Stark calls your hair the Love Canal. You don't
know until you are in college what this means beyond
the sneer in his voice. He still appears in your dreams.
You hope, predictably, for you both to end up in a bar
someday, for him to think you're hot, to hit on you. For
you to walk away.

This is how to make your mother cry:

1. Stop eating.

2. Drink only orange juice.

3. Cut your hair so that she has nothing to braid, so
   that she can no longer say that you look like her.

4. Always answer in English. Even your French is
   better than your Gujarati. She doesn't mean to be
   mean (you understand this), but she laughs and
   you can't stand being laughed at. You stop using
   this other language. Only ha and na. Only kem-
   cho to your grandmothers, on the phone. Only
   tamaro tabyat pani kem cho, to your grandfathers,

and they will answer you in English, perhaps it pains them to hear you slaughter your native tongue like that. Or perhaps they just want you to feel more at ease.

5. Ask her why she left you there. You know why, she will say. I wanted you to learn these things: Bharatanatyam, slokas. She will say: You ask the same things, again and again.

She says, We talked to you every week on the phone.

She says, I mailed you letters, your clothes.

She says, India was farther than it is now. We didn't have the money to just visit. We thought you were happy. You sounded happy. I didn't see my own mother for seven years. Anyway, you can't change schools in the middle of the year.

You didn't see her for seven years, but I was only seven.

You watch her eyes fill.

I know I should have said something. But you—you would have noticed—(Mother)—if I was afraid to walk home by myself, if I squinted at workbook pages, if I inched closer to the TV.

When you are twenty-five, the professor, the one who gave you the wrong prompt, moves to Baltimore. When he is engaged to someone else, someone named Anne or Ann, you return to orange juice. You stop being able to swallow. On your meals of orange juice and coffee and shitty Merlot, you drop to ninety-seven pounds. Boys comment on the lovely articulation of your clavicle bone, on the hollows of your face. Their glance lingers lovingly at your waist—you know they want to gather you in their meaty palms and braille their fingers over the relief of your ribs. You can't seem to get warm and you can't remember things people tell you anymore.

You give *Blue Train* away, along with several clothes and coffee cups. Everything you listen to is *Best of* and on repeat. Your mother is the only one who says: If I could eat for you, I would. Eat, Daughter, eat.

You tell her, I'm only here because you wished for me. You wanted a girl. I know the story; you've told it to me. I can't balance my checkbook. All boys leave for Baltimore. All boys get engaged. Well, did you expect him to wait? She asks. (You only need one, she says, laughing. I didn't even like that one. If he got engaged to someone else, he can't be the right one. Besides, he wasn't even Indian.) Now you're the one crying and this is what you say: I'm no good at cooking. Who will want to marry an Indian girl who hates to cook? What if I made a mistake? Now there is only English on my tongue.

Late at night, you will call Baltimore, ask him why he doesn't love you anymore. He will say, sleepily, that he does. He will move to the next room and he will say that he thinks you shouldn't talk to each other so much anymore. He can see it's hard for you. Years later, this will still embarrass you. Years later still, this might make you mad.

Tell her that you will be fine. (This is never what you say.) She gets on the next bus to Massachusetts. Ten hours later, she is in your apartment. She goes with you to the movie store, where you rent *Pretty in Pink* and *Better Off Dead*. This is what American high school was like, you tell her. But you went to the prom, she says. We let you go, and you had a good time.

She goes to the movie store, and she makes you soup: potatoes and tomatoes and cumin. She goes to the pharmacy and to the store. You take the five pills she gives you and finally you sleep and sleep. You stop talking so much, and you are not so cold, and you sleep.

I liked some boys once, too, she says. Of course, that was before I was married, she says.

You will be fine, she says. I am strong and you will be strong like me. You are my daughter, she says. No one else's. Now both of you have bright eyes. I can teach you, she says, to balance your checkbook. It's not that hard, she says. Cooking is easy, she says. You just have to be hungry. You just have to practice. Hold onto your receipts, she says. I want you to be strong for when I'm gone, she says.

Don't leave me Mom, you say. That's my job, she says. To make you ready. Can you stay a little while longer, Mom. Yes, but get out your bank statements. Let's work on your checkbook, she says. But I want you to understand *Pretty in Pink*. Why? she says. We already watched it.

But did you like it? I want you to like Coltrane. He's saying something important. All that noise. I'd rather talk to you. I could show you how to knit. What's wrong with silence? Nothing nothing, but I like this song. "Afro Blue," it's pretty to me. Maru mathu dukeche. Daughter, my head hurts. If you have to play it, play it low.

letter i never sent

Dear Mr. Bird,

    Are you going to come back here? Sometimes I
just guess. We are going to take my brother to college.
I have bangs now. I can run fast. I dreamt you were my
teacher again.

                  Yours,

                  V.Z.

watch over me; turn a blind eye

He says to me, stay with me, and because he can provide Tampax, two Advil, a glass of water—with ice, though it's not my preference—a clean T-shirt for me to wear (bearing one or another of the names of schools he has attended), I will interpret these gestures, these objects, as able to bear meaning. I will pretend that he will call me to take a walk the next day, or to say hello, or I will pretend that he will call me at all. I will pretend that he means something when he says *You are so beautiful*; that it means anything other than *How do you take this shirt off*. His hands are easy with clips and fasteners, hooks and eyes. He harbors a pile of laundered shirts: frayed collars, folded and stacked. He wears a uniform of flannel, wool, cotton, like every preppy I ever despised; I have to remind myself he is only skin stretched over bone.

He does what it occurs to me that boys do: They are wildly inaccurate metronomes until they are no longer. His hand at my hipbone, this is what moves me. No, I am not kidding. Not his quicker breathing, not his useless metronome. His eyes slightly closed before the quicker breathing.

Before his eyes lightly close, before he snores.

After he sleeps, the alarm clock radio pipes up and his cats jump on and off the bed, the nightstand, the chair on which he hung my shirt, carefully. I wait for him to shut off the music. His cats knock things onto the floor. What could possibly make so much noise, I think. I think I will be waiting a long time. So much noise, but it seems too pathetic to leave now, after all the dancing it took to get me here. In the morning, readying to leave, I see that it was only my earrings, rings that the cats were batting off surfaces before I slept. I kneel down to retrieve my things while he pretends to sleep.

*

As a child, I drank orange juice instead of milk: this is a way of saying no.

If you drink enough orange juice, your bones will stick out of you until they are sharp as keys, until you are mere approximations.

You, Grandfather, always said not to drink water during the evening meal. Not to drink anything.

*

The nicest moment was over at the beginning, as perhaps the nicest moment always is. In the nicest moment, he wants me to stay and I attempt to leave. But maybe none of this has anything to do with what makes the truest moment. In the first moment, back before this moment, we are standing before a stand of trees and we are looking at them, and the way they appear to be everything they are not in the light, in the daytime. Or perhaps we just see what they always are: limbs lighter and darker, trunks shifting, everything finally still. The shadows absorbing us.

In the only moment that ever counted, we are talking about trees. He says: You can see trees better when walking with kids.

I noticed trees with my ex-husband, one I never married, but one who ghosts behind every person I am with and not with now. He is the smell of coffee cooling, of soap and flannel and clove cigarettes; he could be the underside of my name.

He says: You walk next to trees when you need to feel the rootedness, the length of bark, spirit. You see yourself, the I looking at the I, pressing against the bark of a tree. Other times, something breaks, and we try to steady ourselves by walking. Then there is no self commenting upon the self, and isn't that what I'm doing, even now? I hope you might remember a time when you felt the bark beneath your cheek, and leaned even harder, and heard the stream behind the trees, and the stars, even through their death, their dying, appeared somehow brighter.

You said nothing in the most important moments, I suppose, because that is when I tried to hear the river we stood in front of. How it could sound so loud at night, like something breaking, again and again, but in the daytime, blanketed by the things that daytime blankets us with, I had to strain to hear it. And later, when we had sat on his couch, when I came over after I should not have come over, knowing how things might go, how things have a way of going the way they have happened before: still I came over for tea, and it was nearly two in the morning.

It was nearly two in the morning. You had on a tape in Arabic: North African women, crooning. Later you asked what I wanted to hear: I said Bach, I saw you reaching for Miles.

If you drink enough orange juice, your bones will stick out of you until they are sharp as keys, until you are mere approximations.

Grandfather, grandfather, watch over me. Grandfather, grandfather, turn a blind eye.

Some days, I could run a marathon and I walked into a bookstore and bought a hundred dollars' worth of books just because of their names. There was a plan out there and I could see it, finally. Some days I did not leave the house.

Was your courage fashioned from beer? The last time we fell across a couch, a futon (it was my couch last time), he pulled on my hair and I didn't say anything. He dropped to his knees. He said, *You're beautiful*, and I said, *Please. Don't.* I think his was the right move, though; they were the only words I heard him speak, really, once the crooning began.

Grandfather, grandfather, give me strength. Grandfather, grandfather, do not forsake me.

Really, the most beautiful moment, the moment that was beautiful and that can't stay beautiful because of everything that follows and doesn't follow is the first moment where the space between us begins to take on measurement, and either or both of us are noticing how far we are sitting apart and how many pillows are or are not between us. Or maybe that is just math, calculation, the mere weighing of probabilities: will what has happened before happen again? What is most important, our hands before they even touched, our hands when they had touched, but not tangled in the most obvious way, the obviousness of entanglement, of sex, of any human touch the least appealing to me, the part I wish I might forget. What I might hope to remember is how our hands curved around each other. I saw the curve in (y)our thumb and the lamplight lit up my thumbnail till it glowed.

The best part, the only part that I want to remember, is the dusty box of Tampax he presented me with. It left a mark on my sweater that I noticed when he left the bathroom and then it was just me, holding a box of tampons, which his old girlfriend had left. Later I wondered if it was unusual to have things like that still in your bathroom. Would I have kept Old Spice in my bathroom, or even Brylcreem? Of course, these are things my father used, not any boyfriends. Would I have kept Brut, in its dark green bottle, its silver necklace dangling around its throat like a shield, like a threat?

How could a box of Tampax be the best part? How would you tell this story? I don't think this is what you would remember. I don't think I will let you speak.

We talked about tampons because you wanted me to stay. Let me turn you into the third person; this is too difficult. Because he wanted me to stay. He wanted me to stay, and besides the host of other reasons, I had this one.

I said, *I need to go. Let me let you get to sleep.* No. I said, *I should let you go to sleep* or: *Go to sleep* or: *Get to bed.* (Why had you never asked me to stay before? Who were you trying to forget now? Why would you never stay over at my place?) (I can't bear to hear the answer to these questions.)

What I needed to say was this: *I need to go to sleep. I'm leaving now. Let me be your phantom shadow, let me be your ghost: Let me expect back from you what I gave to you. Being present. I can see the time and it's past the time I can be out. My parents are waiting up for me. I am waiting up for me.* (Even if I liked that you asked me to stay, that you needed me, that you seemed to need something, that we could sleep like trees, which have grown up next to each other, tangled together, who have known each other since birth or at least age five. And isn't that love?)

But we know how this will end, and I will write about it afterwards. I should have sat in the wicker chair if I meant to leave. Couches and midnight mean only one thing. Jazz: it can mean only one thing. Tea: if it's two o'clock and he's having his fifth Corona—it can mean only one thing.

Grandfather, grandfather, when will I see you again?

Last year, when the ex-husband left me in the most final way, he stopped measuring the space, and even though we only talked every other week, it was clear the keening had quieted, and I watched the parabola turn into a different figure, into a sine curve, into a line bisecting a quadrant, and he stopped complaining about his girlfriend, stopped talking of when he'd come visit and what he'd drink, where we'd go, what we'd do, how we'd do it. Then I became the orange juice girl; then, then my grandfather came and visited me. He was tall like a tree, not stooped, stopped as he became in the later years, when he asked me, *Do you understand what I'm saying and who are you?*

I was not his first granddaughter, I was not a boy, I was the second child of his first son. Maybe he forgot about me sometimes. I knew only the power of skinny girls. I was the skinniest girl. I would fast like every *Amar Chitra Katha* book I ever read: I had been waiting for a boon.

I fasted with orange juice and kept his Nehru hat by my bed. I watched from my couch, alone, to see if the configurations of the roots had changed (I could see the pine tree from there, and I knew it was you; you had already visited me in a dream). Checked the pinecones, the acorns, any realignment of feathers. I buried the small mouse left in the night and placed three stones to mark the grave. You had appeared and I knew that I had to be vigilant or I might miss what you were trying to say. I kept your Nehru cap by my desk, drank only orange juice. I wound my arms around trees and held on, could hear the keening rising, the wailing, the storm. The bark beneath my face pressed unlikely letters, previously known patterns into my cheek. I took six baths in one day, filled the tub with leaves and rocks and Epsom salts and spices. I wanted to return to the ocean, I wanted to get cooked.

I wrote on the walls in charcoal because all of the other surfaces could move and then I wouldn't find them. I might not find you. My first memory is of you and me, cleaning what I had written off a wall in the house on Hemingway—the smell of ammonia, you were mad at me (I think you yelled at me), but we worked side by side, with an eraser and a cloth.

This whole story is a lie: It can't even come close. I never even called you "Grandfather." Dada. Da-da-ji. Dada. This is only a story written in English. I am only able to write this story in English.

I know this is not the story you would be telling.

I know this is not the story you would want me to tell.

letter i never sent

Dear Mr. Bird,

    Someone else is my teacher this year. He plays basketball with the boys. I don't see Beth so much anymore. My brother is going to graduate soon. Do you think about us sometimes? Anne Mavromatis and I did our project on ESP. Next year, lactose intolerance or peptic ulcers.

                        ~Sincerely,

climate, man, vegetation

It was our country at night. We were walking toward the water and I could hear the runners beginning to run. We were walking toward the row of cars and soon you would find your car and I would have to find mine. It smelled like summer in the suburbs: rhubarb and forget-me-nots. Day turning into night, and me looking for my car keys, holding you up. You had the look of someone who would later buy apples and forget the loaf of bread. After class, the jangle of car keys, the bloom of sweat between your breasts, across your back like silent wings: this is what I remember.

Do you know that smell? You said it smelled like dill. I said no, rosemary and pavement. You said it smells like water rising. I said thyme, black pepper. You said it smelled like grass. Boiled carrots, I said. Cut grass and carrots.

This was the summer I couldn't get up most days. I saw

you maybe three or four times. You were getting ready to move.

They said it was sciatica, but I knew it started in the brain. My brain was stuck. It said to itself over and over, it smells like the suburbs at night! This made sense to me.

At night, before bed, I read an old world geography book. It is predisposed toward mountains. *Mountains, it says, always stand boldly, form the relief in the landscape.* I read about the vertical distribution of mountain vegetation and the importance of trade. I read that south of the polar tundra is the taiga. Different things grow there. There is no relief.

It was a book from a school district that no longer exists. It was a book that came from a library sale. Of course, the countries had different names.

I see the girl who thinks she looks like you. I used to hate her. I used to try and say hello. Now, she laughs when I pass and I can't think of anything to say. She picks at her hair and laughs and laughs. Her mouth is a blot of lipstick. She is proud of her boyfriend. She shows us a ring of keys, heavy with her keys, heavier with his. Her mouth is bougainvillea: common, red.

It's no one's fault. They said take this pill. This one or that one, two before sleep. Take four: in the morning or at night. It's best to avoid alcohol. May cause drowsiness, nausea, lack of appetite, lack of useful secretions, the presence of useful inhibitions. These things, they said, happen sometimes. There is no relief.

Your husband has finished his degree and you are getting ready to move. I will have to return your black shelves and the lamp that needs rewiring. I used the lamp to hang my hats on. Four hats and three of them are dark colors. Each time we talk on the telephone, words fly faster and faster. I imagine them to be bubbles in water. Each word a country, inhabited and blue. These words: they are nearly beautiful that way.

Dear Shobana,

Friendship is a golden tie which ties two hearts together. If we never break this tie, we shall be friends for ever, even if we are apart.

Withbes
Swarn Bilkhu
Nairobi.

SWARN

chel
e Light

h, and one
s to say the
to say that
at the flash
ery relative
der will find

Richard

letter i never sent

Dear Mr. Bird,

    I think maybe you are not that much older than my brother. He says I am getting older. Do you teach college now? Did you ever think about staying here? I still play the violin. I see Beth Teegarden sometimes at ballet.

> Your former
> student,
>
> VZK

ithaca is never far

The first time I kissed an Indian, it didn't feel like incest and I was surprised. Maybe it was because we had blurred ourselves with cheap white wine in anticipation of the event—I can't speak for him. Sure, I'm the product of two Indians—but one and two generations removed from the unpromised land, from daar-baath-shaak-rotli in the kitchen every night. All the desis I knew were cousins or felt like it. Or they were like me and had a thing for blonds. I couldn't blame them, really—it's hard when you grow up here.

Well, sometimes I blamed them, my desi brothers; the very best-looking ones were always sure to have a tennis player on their arms or behind their parents' backs. I scan the announcements to see if they are marrying these tennis players (and yes, some of them are). And what about me? The boys I go out with are scarecrows: working class Methodists or Episcopalians or rebellious trust fund WASPs. You've seen them around—they have an earnestness around the eyes, a nose like a kid drew it, a

dog they love more than girls, the hope of teaching English in China someday.

Maybe I gave the Indian too much credit, because
he didn't try to tell me stories about women in Rajas-
than, thinly quoting the last article in the *New Yorker* or
the *Times* that had to do with the plight of women or
the horror of arranged marriages (so fascinating!) or
the sanctity of the hymen or the supposed dowry problem. Perhaps he was tired of having such stories quoted
back to him from smart Jewish guys at work or well-
read tennis players anywhere—(airports, bars, weddings,
dates). Maybe I should be telling this story to him and
not to you. I don't mind if you listen, though. You: you
could learn a thing or two.

Obviously he didn't taste like saffron, like turmeric, like
asafetida (such a cliché, so Columbus—). He tasted—
you tasted—like the inside of a wine bottle, the green
neck of a wine bottle. Your lips were surprisingly soft.
You clearly wanted to forget about an old girlfriend and
came quickly, damply, into your corduroys. I was embar-
rassed for you. We were out on a terrace and I wondered
who could see us. If there was such a thing as privacy in
India, I didn't find it. If there is such a thing as divination, I misread it. We drank glass after glass and stayed
outside though the insects hummed incessantly around
our hands, our eyes, the rims of our smudged glasses. A

near-empty carafe stared back at us. I thought: Maybe this is the one.

Maybe I should try telling a more palatable story: about kissing a boy who had skin as brown as my brown skin, who worked in computers, who drank single malt with the guys from work, who listened to hip-hop, who wore a blue shirt the color of Friday casual, the color of prep school cool, the color of ease-in-the-world. Maybe the problem is that *I* read the *Times* article. I thought we might fall in love, marry, have a story to tell our children.

Listen kids: We met on the night train from Bangalore to Madras. Or: We met in Madras (now Chennai), but we first noticed each other on the night train. I pretended to sleep, to ignore the dosa-wallah, the coffee-wallah, the others on the wedding trip. I thought the coffee-wallah would return and he never did. How I wanted you to come to my row of seats and visit! And you did, after a time. Or maybe I should tell our children the truth: I had to come find you. You were talking to the girl with yellow hair, and I thought: *this is it*. You have found your perfect opposite. What could you possibly want with me?

What seduced me? Was it traveling with only one other desi on a trip of Americans and a handful of Europeans? It seemed that you were the only other Indian the way everyone nudged us together, left dinner early, pointed out your virtues, etc.—and of course you weren't the only Indian—we were in the ancestral homeland, after all. More of us than I'd ever seen. Our parents called this place home, perhaps, or had once called it home; we had this small fact in common. And we shared this fact with six million people or one out of six people or something rather unremarkable—maybe only remarkable in its easy probability that two of six million might find themselves staring past a carafe into each other.

Was it that we were going to a wedding? Or that you lived in that mythical city, New York, and that I was the age to be looking for myths—or that you had that familiar deviated-septum desi nose—or that you were South Indian (Brahmin, Tamilian), but didn't seem to hold it against me that I wasn't? Is it too scripted to suppose that brown chases brown? That brown is divinely meant to come together with brown? Where is the divination? Was it too much to hope that a night train from Bangalore to Madras might yield a good story for our children?

I suppose our children are still out there, but have gone on to be born to other people. When I told you I lived in Ithaca, you told me you didn't go further than Dutchess County. (I thought you probably wouldn't make it past White Plains. Why did I kid myself?) It seemed pretty clear. We traded three phone calls and talked once, on my coin. It was the last day of October and kids had long stopped ringing the doorbell. That was all.

Children: your mother's mother traveled from Dar es Salaam to Surat to meet her betrothed—on a boat that made her sick. She sailed a steamboat from one continent to another. Surely you understand why I can't marry your father—for him, Ithaca is far. You wouldn't like a father who cannot travel—who will not travel. How will we show you where you are from? Ithaca, Manhattan, Bangalore, Surat. I wasn't quite honest before. All the desis haven't felt like cousins. I'll keep trying. I just want you to be able to get back to the promised land, when you need to, when this whiteness is too much with you.

Oldest son: How will I be able to force you to take Gujarati lessons if your father is American? Who will remind you to take your shoes off at the foot of the temple when I'm tired and your sister is in my arms? Perhaps it will be your father (thin, holding your hand, I can see that much in my mind) who will drive you to your Gujarati lessons, who will be more fluent than me, who will not mind transatlantic flights nor applying for visitor visas. Perhaps he will keep track of the lunar calendar and will remind me of when the harvest festival and the New Year fall each year—there have been times I've not just forgotten, but not even known. There are times I haven't been a good Indian. I have tried to be a good Hindu, to be your good mother. Each night, I unravel.

Forgive me, beta: I'm trying to make a good decision. I look for your dark-lashed eyes, for your crooked smile, in each face, in every bar, in each setup, trying to find your father, trying to recognize your laughter. How will I know if what you want is to be lighter, to be stronger—is to have a connection to Ireland? How will I know if what you are is half Jewish? My hand falters on the loom. First son: Send me a sign, rent these fictions. What I'm wearing is red. What I'm looking for has already been written. What I can't read splays itself across the sky, nightly.

a brown man in the country of origins. But
he's also a man who straddles divide, he
is a brown NY, does he represent two
esteemable qualities for her.
The inevitability of him is a fairy
tale that there is fate that
brings his _princely_ type to her, in
    mythical city, perfect nose ⟹ the mock
fairy tale continues with the positness
of children coming from this tale.
    Back to reality is that his NY ness will
not allow him to venture to Ithaca,
he is too close to the other, the blond
ness. I feel the flux between
reality of interacting with other and
those desires vs. the unreality of promised
land that can't return to.

I like the pathos (you) lay out there, your writing
is risky, barbs underneath a fleecy texture.

letter i never sent

Dear Mr. Bird,

   Who else from our class writes to you? Melissa Dalzell is the captain of the ski team. Her report was on apartheid. You used to call me pack rat. Mine was on anorexia. I have to apply to colleges soon. I am a little afraid of the South. If I went to Duke, maybe I'd see you again. Are you in North Carolina or South?

                              Yours,

                              VZK
                         (i with a flower)

xylem

After not talking to Melanie Bacon in ten years, I was surprised when she asked if she could stay with me in Brooklyn.

Brooklyn—or anywhere I was in New York would be fine—(I had lived in Queens and Manhattan, too, over the last ten years while in graduate school at Columbia and then as a post-doc in a lab at NYU).

Could we crash with you one night on our way to Mexico? said her email.

Did she say we?

Enough already with the visitors—the British Gujarati-by-way-of-Nairobi woman whom I'd met once at a wedding and whose shopping-and-regret-filled tour of New York City boutiques left me breathless and helping her haul her rectangular bags; the last-minute guests who seemed to be there every other weekend my first two years in the city; I felt I was running a bed-and-break-fast while also working at a nine-to-five and no one's job is actually nine-to-five.

For Christ's sake: I lived in a fourth-floor walk-up; it amazed me when they seemed put off if I asked them to carry their sheets and towels two-and-a-half blocks to the laundromat; it wasn't as though I was asking them to pay for the laundry.

Girl, you are always welcome, I wrote back to Melanie.

Husband: I didn't ask about the we, but I had heard she hadn't married Jim Lazenby, so I thought it must be a new boyfriend or a husband.

I know—it's not horrible, they are just assumptions one makes after thirty.

Just then (I was on email) my roommate walked in.

Knocked, but then same breath, walked right in the way my mother used to.

Let's see, Paisley said. What was I going to say?

My friend Melanie—Mel—is going to visit, I said, striving for both cheery and nonchalant, firm but open.

Nice, Paisley said. When is that—I haven't heard you mention her before.

Oh, I said to Paisley, this is the result of the internet—anyone and everyone can find you. And what I was thinking is that everyone comes back—exes, former camp co-counselors—it doesn't seem possible to lose anyone anymore, and knowing me, you think I'd be happy about that, but I find it bewildering—the lack of loss, the lack of mystery, no more letters sent out to your parents' address, mail forwarded or returned, ADDRESS UNKNOWN, but anyway I haven't seen her in ten years and she's the first person I knew who lived in Brooklyn—and she's not coming alone, but I'll give them my room, I said—and I'll sleep on the couch.

Paisley said, I'll be in Atlanta then, I think. Todd was a relatively new boyfriend, but they were racking up the miles on Delta or whatever Atlanta was the hub for.

Question, she said. When are you away next?

Really, it was a fair question.

See, the walls were thin. New York. It was better for everyone if I could arrange to sleep elsewhere and these days I could.

The problem was Cory wasn't my boyfriend and I didn't always know ahead of time when I might see him. He had recently moved to East Williamsburg/Bushwick/Crown Heights—I couldn't keep track of his house-sitting/couch-surfing ways—hell, I couldn't even keep track of him; he didn't want me to.

Until then and really not for a couple more years, I wouldn't see this as a problem we could not evolve out of.

I was in love with someone who said every summer whenever I saw him (I cannot believe I put up with this)—

V, wear a pretty dress for me, and *You're cute, but you could be cuter and more confident*, and *Of course everyone looks at me when I walk into the room.*

What I needed was a spine or a mirror or a reality check or the ability to deal with sleeping alone or the lack of a possible phone call in that after dinner/drinks/blue hour, when you are back home and not reading, not ready to begin the night rituals—taking off the contact lenses, brushing your teeth, laying out the pajamas (yes, I still did that and I wore them, and this tells you something about the kind of person I was—and am).

Xylem is one of two types of transport tissue in vascular

plants—its main function is transporting water and maybe I was missing the equivalent for people—some sort of integral column, though that sounds like missing a backbone, spine, vertebrae—no one can walk without one, no way I could actually be an invertebrate, though over 90 percent of animal species apparently are invertebrates.

Yes, Melanie will come to visit with Magda, I will find out, her six-year-old daughter, Magdalena, Magda for short, the result of her first two-year marriage to a man she met in Oaxaca.

Zoroastrianism, I will find out, is the subject of her PhD research and I will wonder what took her to Mexico and Iran and to a lover who became a husband and why I have stayed here, bouncing around like a ping-pong ball fallen off a green table—from Brooklyn to Queens and back again, slowing, but not stopping, not gaining ballast, a we, something cumulative, accretion, a name change, a larger set of sheets, semipermanent jewelry, an easier way to say, *We're busy that weekend, sorry; my boyfriend's parents are visiting, but we'd love to meet you out for brunch—I know a great place*, because it's Brooklyn, we're in our early thirties, and the world is full of great places, whether or not you're floating, whether or not spinning, whether or not you've gained an anchor or can transport water or are still untethered, floating.

everybody's greatest hits

We were dancing to Marvin Gaye in my living
        room. That's how you said
you knew where you would sleep. We were
        dancing to CDs you bought in
Thailand. Of course, they were bootlegged—
        Every name was misspelled!

Let's go somewhere together! We'll hand each
        other black sweaters and
malaria pills. We'll go away. A small wedding, a
        large country, a long walk.
South, for loose shirts, custom sewn for pennies.
        North, to practice
a language you haven't used in years. Every
        word when leaving
has direction. Every word when leaving is about
        pointing. Pointing
is always about leaving. Lying is only leaving
        before you go.

Take our daughter. I'd tell her things. Daughter,
    I'd say, you don't have to
have wood floors. Don't listen to those others. If
    fifty-fifty is good enough
for your mother, it's good enough for you. Don't
    wash your hair every day.
Americans are wasteful like that. Who else has
    that kind of water?

Watch the blue circle hovering behind each thing
    a person ever says.
It's the truth-teller. Solder your sentences with
    unnecessary light:
diaphanous, solipsism, hegemony, cataract.

Let's elide the things we won't talk about—
Let's accumulate like horses in the darker corners.

letter i never sent

Dear Mr. Bird,

Do you have any kids yet? Do you still write about Mark Twain? I taught seventh grade one year, too. I saw a pocket watch in the store the other day. I thought of yours. I carry it even though it doesn't work.

Regards,

III.

a girl claws her way out

the granite state

I see you, Jim, at seventeen, on a VHS tape
      transferred to digital, and then my memory.
A New Hampshire quiz show, projected on your
      41st birthday dinner—also your memorial.

The drive back to Rochester, New York from
      your Rochester (NH) is now autumnal
      memory.
Nine hours of traffic on my birthday—the day
      after your birthday, also falls into memory.

We were (are) both Libras. Scales, balanced? Not
      me. No one disliked you in my memory.
Each state has a motto—each state a rock, a bird,
      a flower, a capitol, an archive—memory.

"Live Free or Die" is the easiest—if from New
      England or a writer—to commit to memory.
What is mine? The Empire State is not an image,
      nor anything, to attach to memory.

I knew you best in 2000, before I lost my heart,
    before the towers' museum and memorial.
Empire is a building once tallest, then overtaken
    by towers, falling figures, and now memory.

You were the tallest of *Jim, Will, Brian, Chris, Yago*—
    though 6'6" Dan was taller—one memory.
Another is dancing with you, salsa—our knees
    knocking into one another, my silly memory.

Wikipedia tells me the state rock of New York is
    garnet—dark red—Adirondack memory.
I want to not know the state rock of New
    Hampshire. I do. I carry this memory.

I unearth your workshop comments from a box
    in my parents' basement, doubting memory.
You wrote two pages of comments, your name, then
    one last run-on—now-cherished memory.

I like the pathos you lay out there, your writing is
    risky, barbs underneath a fleecy texture. This
    memory.
I am pleased you call my writing risky. I will
    replace all other memories with this
    memory.

I see you, even younger, on *Granite State Challenge.*
    You guessed wrong, now tender memory.
The celebration, candles lit and held, skits,
    conjuring you, witness!—repository of your
    memory.

My fiancé and I attended—in one day—
    your birthday party—your mass—your
    memorial—
It was your wedding as well—our gathering,
    your reception. I did marry. I carry your
    memory—

the half king

tenth avenue, new york

That last time I was in Chelsea, I walked up and down Eighth Avenue not remembering where the Half King was. I was thirty-nine then, two whole avenues off, trying to remember who I was from that other life: those countries of twenty-two and thirty. I rode the train back to Brooklyn with the rising of a headache so fierce I couldn't look at the ceiling for two days and a boy whose lavender shirt hid an inverted sternum and a string of tattooed words—prayers in various languages. A few days after, talking on the phone to Carrie and she said, Girl. It's Tenth Avenue. Now she has a baby at her hip, a ring that never comes off, a house in Santa Cruz with a view of the ocean. Ten years ago, we both lived here.

everyone talked about leaving.

We grew up within five miles of each other, district lines funneling us into different schools—some to the city magnet and East Side schools and some to the suburbs. They dated each other—the usual rivalries, unrequited loves, triangulations—but I was outside of it. They worked at the India House, one of two Indian restaurants in our city. To me, these kids were uncomplicated and beautiful. They were future or past Zen Buddhists, surprisingly good dancers and good-enough musicians, devoted pot smokers and skiers, the sons and daughters of doctors and lawyers and professors who did not become doctors, lawyers, and professors. They went to community college; they traveled. To them, I had a kitchen that smelled like cumin and a live-in grandmother who cooked. In my town, the sons and daughters of doctors, engineers, and professors replicated, and that was that. To the city kids, I was exotic and amenable. Different town, different skin color. I didn't have a history with them. I was a late addition and the only Indian. We were lithe twenty-one-year-olds when we met—you should have seen us—square teeth, fresh skin, still thin. They had never seen me in braces nor had I seen them. Getting to know them was like going to someone else's high school reunion. Because it wasn't mine, I could enjoy it.

cobb's hill, rochester

Sitting on our hill, looking out at our city—its modest skyline, someone was always smoking, someone else just flicking the lighter's wheel. We were there in every season—watching the birders, the butterflies, the lovers; the kids sledding, the women walking, the men running by listening to their headphones. We sat and talked;

sometimes we kissed. This was all I needed for a while: a hill, a view. We never went to other cities on the weekend; we never went anywhere. New York City was another country, a set of names I didn't know—neighborhoods and subway lines—complaints about the 6 train, the unbearably slow F train—Central Park West, the East Village, Tribeca (whatever these places were)—to use places other than New York—all to show off your cosmopolitan, well-traveled self. It was western New York: disturbingly close to Ohio and six hours from anywhere you wanted to be. It was where I had my first stumbling kiss, drinking Rolling Rock by the littered ditches near the expressway, walking over to Cobb's Hill, too drunk to drive home.

We were young then. Our city, then, had decayed the least of the ones upstate; digital had not yet strangled Kodachrome and the film business. Jobs had not yet migrated overseas. But our time was coming. We made some small accommodations—changed our tagline from the Flour City (mills on the high falls of the Genesee River) to Flower City (lilac trees every shade of purple) to the Image City. Xerox, Bausch + Lomb, Kodak: every major industry was ocular, but we did not see fast enough or far enough. And half of us had not yet moved to California. And the musicians and dancers had not yet left for New York. And I had not yet begun to think I could, too. I think I was happy in some absolute, unspeakable way, though. I can't remember if I knew it or if it has just become something to say now: *I was happy then.*

twenties

I was twenty-two then. By twenty-five we had all moved. The people who stayed explained themselves when we ran into them at the old bars on Alexander Street and the new bars on South Avenue. We never asked, they always told: they had spent a year (eight months) somewhere else. San Francisco, Chicago, Tampa, Boston; they mentioned the independent film theater and the cheap rent here in town. But they were sheepish, the way I had been, when I moved back and taught at the middle school in the center of town. Even my old teachers said, What are you doing here? One of my history teachers, the curly-haired, kind-eyed track coach, took me aside and said, This is what I make now. This is what I'll make when I retire. You will make even less. He gave me his son's business card and said his company was hiring.

And so I moved. If you had any ambition (and I had enough), you had to leave. The easiest way to break up (for example: with the Irish kid I kissed occasionally then) is to move away. I spent the second half of my twenties single, waiting for I don't know what. Some sort of sign to bring me back. I couldn't take New York seriously—haircuts more expensive than most clothes I owned, interns with interesting glasses working for no pay, strivers. I just assumed that I would circle back to find a boy about my age from my previous life, waiting for me. The whole point was to recognize him.

summer camp

The Half King is one of those new old-seeming hip bars. Leaded-glass windows; one cadmium-orange wall, sponge-painted so you can see the pale showing through; booths and bar and floors built from wide, weathered boards of pine and oak. This city is full of such bars; maybe all cities are. One night, curious about the name, I leaned over the bar using what little cleavage I have. The second bartender made his way over. He can't say much and it's loud anyway. They were appealing to our demographic: seventies classic rock. People are wearing deliberately faded T-shirts in blue and green announcing the names of places, as though they are the names of teams. Minnetonka, New Jersey, Canada: the usual irony. It was happy hour in Chelsea; the art opening after-party, gallery-goers loud and getting louder, still hungry, already a little drunk on wine and cheese cubes, on wilting celery sticks and broccoli florets. The predictable effect of grazing on food that will leave you hungrier than when you began.

The bartender says: All the wood in the bar comes from a two-hundred-year-old barn in Pennsylvania. Why? I didn't ask. He tells me that the Half King was a Seneca chief, part of the Iroquois, who ended up in the Ohio Valley. I wonder if they have to memorize this. He points me toward a plaque, black letters on gold, lit by one perfect light curving above it, on the far wall:

> "The eighteenth-century Seneca chief known as the Half King is a figure so obscure that no one knows his real name—it was most likely Tanaghrisson, or something close to it. Little is known of Tanaghrisson's early life."

The plaque and the story are both out of the way and also highlighted. I add this to the information I know: The Iroquois or Haudenosaunee were the Six Nation confederacy in Upstate New York. They spread out along the Finger Lakes, west to Lake Erie. We memorized this in Social Studies. None of us escaped going to some sort of camp named after the tribes: Seneca, Oneida, Onondaga, Cayuga, Mohawk. The last tribe, the Tuscarora, did not have a camp or lake named after them (they were not local to the area). My street was once Seneca land and does it matter here, here in this city, where everything new refers to something else that was once before? My entire neighborhood: All of it belonged to the Seneca. There is a plaque near the elementary school that tells us so. Our streets were a series of British-sounding names. Rochester is where I was once asked if my father was an Indian chief. Wrong kind of Indian. Wrong kind of chief. Chief of Cardiology, asshole.

The plaque near our elementary school was just another story about another chief: another agreement, conditional, and later broken. Tanaghrisson. What does it mean if nothing is known about your early life? Why is nothing known?

bartenders, younger than you, chelsea
The first bartender I try to shove my way close to does not look at me for a while. She has three tattoos I can see, wears olive cargo pants and a tight black shirt that hikes up to show her abdomen. She is young enough to sport one that is smooth, flat, unmarked. She looks Indian. She wears a nose ring, her hair in two flat, shiny braids, and a bangle tightened across her left biceps. Ink-blue script decorating the nape of her neck and she's talking to the other two bartenders; they are passing by each other on the way to glasses, to lime triangles, to the cash register. They have a language back there behind the bar, it's seamless almost, a silent dance, and I can imagine them drinking after hours, after the rest of us have stumbled home. I wonder if she's the kind of girl Mark would like. I wonder if she's the kind of girl I should try to look like. She and I and a couple of others are the dark in a sea of white. This bar could be Upstate. Mark. He is not even looking over at us.

Hey, sweetie, she says to me. What can I get you? I'm taken aback by her use of the diminutive. I'm clearly older than she is. Seeing how crowded the place is, skimming the labels and names, I say, quickly, Whatever's good on tap. I don't want to make a decision; I let her decide.

bad indian food

The first time I saw Mark, we were in Chelsea. A bunch of us were meeting at the Half King after Carrie's opening. I had dinner first, a date, at an Indian restaurant with jewel-colored drinks that looked better than they tasted. This place showed sixties Bollywood films with the sound turned off. The women danced on the screen above the bar, and I could look up between first-date questions to see their silent singing. Do you like to travel? I was waiting for the rain scene, for the translucent soaked white sari, for the male lead to pull her close. How many brothers and sisters do you have? I was with the last in a string of nice but obviously wrong guys. I've always wanted to go to Spain. He paid for dinner and then we walked some blocks over to the Half King. He left me at the door of the bar, had to work early the next day. I had not encouraged him to come inside. It's loud, I said. Thanks for dinner. I had a good time, I said, and smiled. I wore jeans that felt too tight, which meant they fit. And it meant that I was, in my own way, trying to take the date seriously.

twenty-nine, brooklyn

After this last date with another nice guy, I went back to seeing the slackers I called my friends. Mark was not my friend, but we had friends in common from Rochester. It bothered me that you could see the same people at parties for years and never make that leap from friend-of-friend to friend. I have always had a willful persistence to want what isn't there.

zip codes, elvis costello

We went to different high schools, lived in different towns (I would rather say that than admit where I lived. I had a city zip code). Mark showed up at the same places on Monroe Avenue, before Monroe burned out into a Mediterranean restaurant and two diners, that secondhand store and a Hollywood Video. Five blocks of the Avenue succumbed to chains—as if to a fire or an illness. This was before all the preppies had their noses pierced, before they all had tattoos. Mark has glasses now, hair spiked, a sort of Elvis Costello look. It's not that he looked like him exactly; it's that sense of someone. Year later when we run into each other in the city, it's at a lounge in Park Slope with dark velvet curtains in the back, a fake fireplace, and I play—unoriginally—Journey on the jukebox.

twenty-five, rochester

The Irish kid, the seventh grade teacher, grew up in Utica, so for him Rochester was big enough. He had

cowlicked brown hair, bright blue eyes, and a Filipina
ex-girlfriend. So he, like most of us, had the desire to step
out of his own life. He liked his apartment even though it
was across the street from a cemetery, next to a loud bar
and a flower shop. I didn't like his apartment (bachelor
beige, an overstuffed sofa from his brother, an oversized
picture of his mother), but I loved the cemetery. It was
the best one in the area for walking, and Frederick Douglass and Susan B. Anthony were buried there.

Like every kid who grew up there, I knew about Susan B.
and could recite the local attractions, but I've never seen
the grave. I didn't know about Frederick Douglass until
I moved back; suburban social studies curricula forgot
him, which shouldn't surprise me, but still does.

After we broke up, the teacher got himself a good
camera (this was the late nineties, long before digital)
and started taking black-and-white photos of headstones
and trees and epitaphs and sky. He refused to speak to
me at school. I couldn't stand being ignored. We chap-
eroned a school trip to Canada, Quebec City. No words.
He looked at me. *What is it that you want?*

I tried to forget he had come to our first date with a rose
in hand. Who does things like that anymore? It must
have suffered, wilted in its green wax paper on the table
at the India House, while we sipped our mango lassis.

But still. I wrote a letter to him. I called a few times. I didn't want to let it go.

Emerson says: "When the half-gods go, the gods arrive." Even the wrong ones: I didn't want to let them go.

q train, brooklyn bridge

That night they were in Chelsea at Carrie's show, then at the Half King, sliding into a wooden booth. Mark came from deejaying somewhere. We always sit the farthest away from each other at these things. Later, I knew he would return to Brooklyn to some other underground party. I was more than slightly jealous. He had prematurely gray hair and a place in Brooklyn Heights. It wasn't clear to anyone how he afforded it. And maybe that made it clear.

There had been a girlfriend, but I hadn't heard anything about her for a while. I hated those guys who were not single, but their girlfriends were never around. I was younger then. I didn't understand why you'd be out without your girlfriend. Every one of these guys were bike riders, had the sheen and stink of sweat, a surety that allowed them to disdain deodorant and to dodge cars and cross bridges, suspended over water on two wheels at night. I followed that certainty then. When I first got to New York, everything about it disoriented me. Crossing the river on the Q train, on the

Manhattan, I watched the pillars of Brooklyn Bridge and was soothed—the bridge belongs to everyone. But beyond that, at night, there were too many bridges to keep straight, at least after three drinks, at least when I was waiting for a cab, at least when I was new to New York. The bridges looked like strands of diamonds to me then. I didn't need to know where they went. I didn't care. I was happy just to see them.

I think about this. It seems as if there is something about us that we ourselves can't see that lets everyone know where we are from. At the end of the night, Carrie walks me to the door. Are you OK to get home?

What's OK, I said. I felt reckless from beer, reckless from the city. Sure, I said. I miss you. Even when you're here, I miss you. You look good, she said, and squeezed my hand. Her hair was long and loose and she looked beautiful, even with half her makeup worn away, only the ghost of lipstick on her lips, a smudge of lavender above her eyes, traces of blue eyeliner underneath.

carrie, new york, leotards

At the Half King, it was smoky—this was before the city put the ban into effect. Too much music, girls crammed into their tops, hair straightened, drinks brimming, nearly pushing over. I didn't believe in hair straightening then.

I didn't believe in silver shirts, but it was all I wanted. To be that obviously the center of the room, garish, shimmering. Most of my twenties, I wondered why I was single, but by thirty I had figured out that most of being pretty was merely agreeing that you were.

The shirt I wore was turquoise, reliably striking against brown skin. Guys: It's not difficult to get their attention. You just need something sparkly, some color. Mark nodded in my direction: he almost never said my name. Sometimes I wondered if he actually knew it. We showed up at the same birthday parties and readings, knew the same people who had worked at the same restaurants in college—the seedy Brazilian restaurant, the mediocre Ethiopian place on Alexander Street that seemed always about to go out of business. The food was awful—it seemed as though someone got sick every other time we were there—but somehow it never stopped us from going, and the place never closed down.

Carrie could slip us free drinks. This is not a small thing: to have a place where the bartender lets you run up a tab that you will never pay. Carrie wore those fitted tops that make you think of leotards, scalloped across her chest, long blonde hair slightly tangled. She took dance classes (we all did then). All the girls I knew were dancers; all the boys we knew were in bands.

mark, skinny ties

Something changes when someone says your name. I almost never said his name, either. I thought I should dislike him, because I wasn't sure he liked me. But really, it made me want to try harder.

He dressed ironically, which sometimes I liked, other times felt too old for. I wasn't living in Williamsburg and had never really wanted to. I liked the expression on his face: rueful, ironic. Three days' growth. But his suit: That's what got me. Polyester—the whole ensemble. Gray, with a tie (skinny), matte, the way you'd want to see it. Black plastic frames. Fabulous, without trying. He'd gotten it right, and I suppose that's what I liked.

outside

Mark says, So, you're going back to school? What do people do with a degree in cultural studies these days? There are no jobs out there. Carrie is my number one. She says, You don't know what you're talking about. We'll be going to her book parties. You don't need to go to school to write a book, Mark points out, raising his eyebrows.

The only way to end this conversation is to drink more, or to leave, or to kiss someone. All the usual and customary ways of dealing with boredom or anxiety.

The booth behind us cheers, on their way to or just

after a round of shots. I kiss Carrie, somewhere between mouth and cheek, and place my hands on her head. Not everyone loves me as much as you do. It's one of many reasons I like to be around her.

I'm going out for a smoke, Mark says. My cigarettes are in Chris's car. Chris tosses him the keys. I press my way past the other people so that I can leave, too. It had been an invitation. Carrie says, Do you want me to go with you? No, I tell her. I just need to get some air. And it's true—the number of people has tripled—and I feel as though I'm at a terrible college party and I want to leave.

Our booth: They were slackers and they were my friends. Some of them, like Mark, I hadn't known in Rochester. We met in the city then traced our lives back to the neighborhoods circling Cobb's Hill and our birthright: the ability to deal with weather. We made allowances for each other; proximity, having grown up near each other, seemed to mean something once we had all left that area. History = destiny. Does it? Now thirty, we were dancers teaching Pilates and yoga, we had dropped out of graduate school to be in bands. We were temping our way through offices in Midtown, filching paper supplies, drinking too much with bartender-actors who talked much more than acted. I wrote a little, drank wine in plastic cups at other people's readings, dragged student essays in my wake. We lived in Greenpoint, Washington Heights, Inwood, Bushwick. At twenty-five, you could find us on the Upper West Side and Park Slope. After thirty, it was harder to live like that, three to a place, just for the neighborhood.

Do you want a smoke? Mark held out the package. I have always envied smokers—they have a way out of every situation, a chance to look back at whatever moment, even in a party, and see it as a scene. Sure. I don't smoke, really, unless I've had a couple of drinks.

How's that law school thing going? I say.

I hate it. I'm not going to practice. I just wanted to have done it.

You don't want to practice at all?

It's its own thing, just going to law school. That's been interesting, an exercise, you know. Like Sudoku or training for a marathon. But lawyers are fucking boring.

Yes, I wanted to say, I know you are smart. Do you think you might move back? I'm always thinking about it— and that separates us—divides those of us at the booth that night. The ones who consider going back and the ones who never would. The ones who were all about getting out. It doesn't matter that you can own a house, a three-story Victorian, there. You'd still have to live there—that's the point. No place there is even close to the bars in Chelsea except maybe that place down on Monroe. The independent bookstores had disappeared: the lesbian one, the rare books one, the general one— all of them—replaced with only a drug store and a video store—we were renting movies and filling our Lexapro and Paxil scrips more than reading; the adult movie theater was still open, and so was the ethnic clothing store where we all worked at one point or another. Mark once said that New York spoils all other cities for you. But I am not him.

We are running out of things to say. I am shaking; it's February and it's cold out. Not upstate-cold, but cold enough. Mark leans over to me. You're cute, he says. Don't you have a girlfriend? I ask. Relax, he says. It's just a compliment. You're cute, too, I say, but it falls flat. It was just a moment and I hadn't needed to make it visible. So many things, I've come to believe, are better left unsaid. I want that moment back, back at the bar, when the current starts to snake between us, the press of people between us, but we are angling toward each other by talking to everyone else.

So what's your book about? Mark asks. I hate this question. It's like *The Great Gatsby*, I say, except set in western

New York instead of Long Island and Manhattan. Mark takes another drag from his cigarette. He doesn't know me well enough to gauge whether or not I'm kidding. So are you Jordan? he asks. Tennis is for assholes, I tell him. Daisy Buchanan? He's showing off now. I don't believe in affairs, I say. Mark takes another drag from his cigarette, looks toward the West Side Highway, eyes closed. Then he unzips his jacket, begins digging into his pocket for his phone. I hear the ring, distorted from clothing and the honking of cars, but it sounds first farther and then so close, as though he is a moving car and the sound is blaring from the speakers. It sounds like a Prince song, but it could be anything. I walk over to Tenth Avenue, just a few steps away. I've left my phone inside and there's nothing for me to do with my hands.

This isn't what I thought thirty was going to look like. Everyone always reaching for something else. Almost none of us wears rings—that kind of ring.

Mark comes up next to me so quietly that I jump. It's just me, he says. It wouldn't be *The Great Gatsby* if it were in western New York, you know. Yes, I say, irritated. I know. I'm the English teacher here. I take a deep breath and hold it for a moment before exhaling. Mark says, I need to get something from Chris's car. I watch my breath smoke away and then follow him around the corner.

boat.

We've walked back inside. This bar: We could be anywhere—Cleveland, Milwaukee, upstate along the
Hudson, a million college towns, even Rochester—once
the art crowd disappears. We could be at home. I am
a loud person trapped in a shy person's mannerisms.
Things had gotten a little quiet out there, and cold.

Carrie says, V, come sit next to me. She looks tired, mas-
cara shadows beneath her eyes, lines at the corners showing her age—the blondes, it seems, were getting them
first. I look over at the long bar and it punches me in the
stomach—the knowledge of how much I want to be the
twenty-three-year-old with the cut arms behind the dis-
tressed wood, of how much I want to be someone other
than me. If I squint, we can all be on a boat—all the
wood is old and gorgeous—and we're off the coast near
Woods Hole, heading to Bermuda or Barbados. Carrie
asks, What are you looking at? I open my mouth, about
to launch into how I miss my younger self, how I want
to be that girl with the flat abdomen, how I want to find
someone who I can move back home with. If you're with
someone, you can go back.

I stop myself. They've written the alcohol percent-
ages next to the names of the beers. I point toward the
old-fashioned black chalkboard above the bar where
the names of both bottled and on-tap beers are listed.

In small, neat letters, next to the beer, alcohol content is listed—4.8, 8.5—as though they are scores. Isn't that strange? I say. Carrie looks up and beyond the crowd of people.

What? she says. It's gotten so loud now. Who do you think is cute? *Who is winning*, I think. She brushes her hair away from her face, but one strand stays, slightly stuck there by sweat. Her lipstick is almost completely erased now, but it doesn't make her any less pretty. She likes to play this game as though she is single, too.

school

The seventh grade teacher married his student teacher and moved to Canandaigua, the westernmost of the major Finger Lakes, once also Seneca land. Canandaigua means "the chosen spot" in Seneca. The Seneca's word for themselves is Onöndowa'ga. It means people of the Great Hill. The words we use for ourselves are always different than what other people use. How could it not be? But still. Something always gets lost.

The teacher had a baby and a weekend band. He had gotten over his first engagement and he had gotten over me. I let him find out from other people that I was leaving. I had never planned on staying. Not unless he was remarkable. (Was I that much of a snob? I was.) I wanted remarkable. I wanted more.

I'd already gotten accepted to a master's degree outside of the city (yet another program, the easiest way to leave). School was the way I always left: an orientation, a start date, a move in a certain direction, parental approval. Now I was leaving again, another program, another state, another degree, so every place, everything I did, had that clarity—I wanted to remember, to fix things into place. That is what leaving does. That is what I've become addicted to.

We walked outside because we could. Mark said I want to kiss you because he could. I said, Aren't you living with that girl?

organic farming and acupuncture

Carrie says, What about Chris? Chris has been quietly talking to someone's roommate and looks up to see if anyone needs a drink. He is marriage material, wearing a button-down, a watch, and a smile that is guileless. I want to get married, but not to that. Not now.

Carrie's boyfriend used to date someone else at our table, a redhead whom I hadn't known. She's married now, has the proud early bump, a white eyelet blouse, fitted to show off the swelling. I'm older than she is. The redhead majored in anthropology but knew enough not to go to graduate school in it. She lets you know she traveled to Haifa and Lesbos, went on archaeology digs—that she has a rent-controlled apartment on the Upper West Side decorated with fossils; that she worked at the Smithsonian before she got tenure in a suburban school district. Her husband inherited some money; they have a place three hours away, upstate.

Carrie leans over to me. We're thinking about getting pregnant, too, she says to me. It's a mix of shy and confident—the way she says it. We are still too young then to know better, to have friends who take Clomid and see acupuncturists, who cannot bear to attend other friends' baby showers. She talks about organic farming and massage therapy school. I smile at her. When she says we, what opens up is what was always there: a person, a house, a plan behind her. Always that almost-jealousy between friends. What about you, she asks. What about me?

new york

Carrie and her boyfriend have known each other since high school. I'm jealous of that. It's what I always wanted. But I also can't imagine it. What's the point of paying the rent to live in New York if you've already met someone? New York is about looking around. New York for me was about looking around. Mark slides back into the booth. I ask Carrie's boyfriend if I can buy him another drink. He says no, I elbow my way to the bar, push in front of the frat boy wall, and come back holding two Coronas.

I was always a shy person hiding behind a loud person's mannerisms. The people from my high school I would long for if I let myself long are long married. That's what people in my town did—replicate and duplicate and pro-create. I have done none of the above. I want to wear something so bright and so tiny that the wall of people will part. I bring back one Corona to push across the table, one for me to clasp my fingers around. I ease my way back into the booth and look at all of them—the ones I know and the ones I've just met. The roommate dragged along, another friend of a friend, whose name I don't remember five minutes after we were introduced. Chris, who looks like a nice guy, a guy my mother might like, and who looks at me as though he might be inter-ested, if I were to look back.

I can already tell I will remember this moment. I can't stay here at thirty, stay living in a room with an airshaft window, stay living in a place where the boys who ask me out will never help me move when I am actually moving. Carrie says: Why do you waste your time with the kind of guy who won't help you move? What about one who will pack up his crummy car and move with you? The kind of guy I should want probably has a nicer car than that. And he probably has a better job than me, a good job even, so I am the one who would have to move. Or maybe it's not about jobs at all; maybe it's about being willing to stay.

It's not like I have someone like you do, I say. A Boyfriend. Most of the time, I can't even say the word. I can say: This guy. I can say: The DJ, The Nice Guy, The Seventh Grade Teacher. The Pot Dealer, The Assistant Professor, The ER Doctor. Someone is driving Carrie home. And he, her boyfriend, is the tallest and the best-looking guy there. I didn't say it before, but it's true. The only people who have ever helped me move share a last name and some amount of genetic material with me. Mark has a girlfriend, Carrie says. I know, I tell her. We were just talking.

When I leave the Half King tonight, it will be just me on the sidewalk, flagging down a taxi. After thirty—I can see it—the world is Noah's Ark. And even if Carrie walks outside with me, I will be the only one getting into the car. I have no idea what kinds of deals have been brokered between the people who sit here, grinning and shit-faced, who live with each other, whether or not there are rings or merely the promise of them, or no promise at all.

I know it's hard sometimes, she says. It would be for me,

too. It's not so bad, I say, to sleep diagonal on the bed. I get the whole thing. Anyway, I have you, I tell her. And that's not a small thing.

I want to believe Carrie, who is across from me, absently rubbing a turquoise pendant and leaning into her boyfriend's shoulder. She thinks I can be like her. That I could have chosen differently, that I could choose differently. I want to be more than someone's cigarette break. I want to have a friend where it's not necessary to lie. I want to be able to say something to her that she won't say to her boyfriend without my asking her not to say anything.

Carrie notices Mark's arm nearly touching mine. He's someone else's, she says, after he's gotten up, and looks at me, hard. I notice her cheeks are flushed, but it takes me a minute to realize she's angry. And then another moment to realize that I am, too.

We were once twenty-one and not married, we wore pink and peach tank tops and loose Indian skirts. We were not married; we flit around the room and boys as though we were butterflies. We were butterflies; we were twins. Now she is a plant, planted, an aloe vera or jasmine, blooming. Maybe a begonia or a geranium, potted, a houseplant, domestic.

He's not wearing a ring. I open my eyes, try to look aggrieved, can meet her eyes, but not stay there for long. Carrie, I say, and shrug my shoulders. I have not signed a lease with anyone else. I have not promised anyone anything. She has known Mark longer than she's known me; why shouldn't she be looking at him and talking to him.

My dinner date was a nice guy. No, it wasn't a great date. It really wasn't. And he is not at this booth, right now. He could be, but I would not be the single girl at the table, aggrieved, if he were there.

Mark is lighter now and I'm heavier—because I wanted nothing before—and I want him now. I want him to look at me. I want him to call me. I want it to be OK that I took his phone, dropped it on the ground. That the ground opened up, and the phone split apart, bounced away from us on the sidewalk. That our hands touched when we both bent down to retrieve the battery. That I reached up to his shoulders and that I let him pull me to the back of the building. I want it to be OK that I walked us over to his car. This could be a different story. He could want to move away with me. We could tell a story to our children or at a wedding.

If I have one more drink, this is what I'll see: Those of us who want to stay a little longer, stretch it out, this night, who have some reason not to want to leave right away, and those who can let it go, see it's just another night in a set of nights like this. Someone's birthday, someone's art opening, someone's dance performance downtown, and we're out afterwards. I catch myself watching the beautiful bartender again—I can't tell if she's twenty-two or twenty-seven—if she's from Ohio or from Scarsdale or from Bergen County. I can't hear the mid-Atlantic vowel shift in her voice since what we are doing is not talking, we are observing, we are interpreting. What she has is something I wish I had had. The knowledge that it is OK to use the fact that you're young and reasonably pretty. Now I see that I was using it all along. I used to be afraid to hail a taxi, but the truth is that if I hesitated, someone else would step up to hail it for me.

My hands are cold, and I place them over the tea light flickering on the table. What I have is an address book full of half kings—people I once loved. People I still love. None of them are here at this table. Even those of us who are here: We can barely hear each other across that table.

back

I sit there, stay, hand curved over the tea light, for another hour or two, trying to fix it all into place. I am making a picture to conjure for when I'm missing New York. Lime wedges suspended in Coronas; strings of white Christmas lights; still-skinny ex-dancers; wooden booths scratched over with names, circles and circles of rings, staining. The archaeologist, drinking her seltzer. Postcards advertising lipstick or bands sticking for a moment to the bottom of our half-drained bottles before falling to the table. My blue shirt, the smell of smoke, the profile of Tanaghrisson on the far wall.

I want to know the correct spellings and the preferred names. Another common spelling is Tanacharison. Growing up, we learned Iroquois. Now, it's Haudenosaunee. I learn everything late. Maybe we all learn everything late.

I'm buying another round. I'm looking around. Everything I can see clearly is about to pass. I'm leaving, I say.

I know tomorrow is another bad hangover waiting for me, but right now, the bar slowly clearing, the air outside sharpening, I can believe that the candle heating my hands, the oceanic shush of highway, our tangled arms and legs—that all of that is enough (and that I will grow out of it)—the car outside, wanting Mark.

I tell myself I can move back, that New York isn't a river, rushing. And none of this lasts anyway—not Carrie and me in a twin-way, not Mark and me, not twenty-one, not the possibility of Chris or any other nice guy smiling at me across the booth. Not what I want most of all: a bouquet of possibilities, the ship—which was once something else—choosing to return. This time he would choose differently—and I tell myself after thirty, so will I.

letter i never sent

Dear John:

I looked for you on the computer. I am in graduate school now. If you looked me up, you'd find lots of people who are not me. No one's name is only. Do you still play the guitar? I haven't seen Beth Teegarden in a long time. I don't wear glasses anymore. What if I saw you again? I think I am pretty much the same.

Your student,

_____   _____

skeleton, rock, shell

Shells are chiefly protective and skeletons are mainly for support. Skeletons are, therefore, chiefly internal structures, whereas shells are external. In some animals the same structure may serve both as a shell and a skeleton . . . Every animal with a shell, for example, must, at least in theory, decide whether a light but mobile shell is better than a heavy but immovable one. A shell may provide some protection, but it requires energy to construct and move; animals without shells save energy but are vulnerable to their enemies.

—William Lee Stokes in *Essentials of Earth History: An Introduction to Historical Geology*

I once knew a man who told us to listen to the spirits inside stones. He held a rock in his hand. Think, he said, of what this rock has been through. How it has traveled.

I imagined the pressures of his hand.

I ignored the rest of the lecture, the importance of fossil fuels, and thought instead of my once-long hair.

Here is the whorl of a fingerprint, the loneliness of a shell.

Stones speak, he said, if you close your eyes and your mouth; if you listen. I crossed and uncrossed my legs. I leaned, tossed my hair, and enacted the look of the slightly bored: allowing the look of possible future intelligence to sprawl across me. After the lecture, when the others had collected their satchels and book bags, their long, red scarves; after they had filed out toward the glass-front dining halls and the miniature town, I stayed behind. I stole that rock he had left on the wooden lectern. I went home to my dorm room, the weight of the rock in my jacket pocket like a secret leaning, a weight pulling me in one direction, and I walked perhaps overstraight to compensate.

I want to say that I got to my room and closed the door.

That I silently pried the clothes off my body. I lit candles and incense (the only law I broke repeatedly, besides speeding) and that I balanced the stone on my stomach. That my hip became a sand dune. That the rock, feeling smoother as it passed over each bone, as it sloughed off cells—that this stone enraptured me. That it cleansed

me. I lay in the bath, the water beginning to cool. I
want to say that the weight of this rock succored me.
I felt the boy parts of me: my hips, the buttons of my
spine, percussing each notch of the sternum, as though
my body were something I could unhook and step out
of, and sometimes I did dream of this. Unhooking. The
O'Keeffe of me. The body a dress I had grown tired of.
I wanted to see my bones. I wanted to loosen my skin
until I could see underneath. I wanted to return to bone.

Words conjure. Why not simply say it? The only oracle
is in the bones, is in the pattern of what is left. Of what
remains.

I once drank too much. I was not in a ceremonial way.
I danced and danced. I wanted to erase you. Ease you
into the sack of memory; any kind of regret, rising. This
is the oracle of the bones. I drank so much I could not
remember. I drank so much I could not push him away.
I could say now: I didn't mean to. I could say: I tried
to get warm, to dislodge you, a slow suddenness now
sealed in my skin. A rock is a planet fallen to earth. I
drank coffee after coffee, re-fastening my head, shaking
my head from side to side, gingerly, like something that
had once been whole.

I wanted to sleep and I wanted to not remember: aren't
these the most elemental of human wishes? I am no

different. He stopped my mouth with his finger. It is an unheated attic and it is nearly December. I will have to remember this night until I can forget this night. I want to forget your hands. The deftness of your hands. The yellow-haired girl crying by the door. I hadn't seen you in eight or nine years. You were *engaged* the last time I saw you.

Any child, walking along the shore, will fill her hands with shells. Sand from her hands, spilling from the corners of her dress, pulled up. A fist of the rocks that looked green in water. What is there left to do but throw them out when you return home?

Arrange the broken pieces you carried back.

We dream space until shapes emerge: a wheel, mandala; confetti.

Loss is the name for the Spanish settlers who could not forget.

You say it was a misunderstanding. You say you had no idea. (I seemed to be pushing back against your pushes, perhaps the organism of me was; my body moving in the way it understood that movement begins. And ends. Betrayal: a response you cannot control. To an action you cannot control.) Bones are the only oracle.

Your hands were so quick; nimble. Cut the hands off of quick boys. The boy with quick hands jumped over the small brown girl. She never found her earrings. They got lost like I wish you had got lost. Get lost in the world. Get me out of this world.

I will whittle myself to the bone. I will triangulate. All the more to be invisible from you. All to disappear into the farthest corner. All to ruin. All to invite ruin. What else will last? In the divine way, I mean.

A rock is a desire fallen to earth. You throw your hands up, in the practiced way. A rock is a planet that has begun to divine, a planet chipped to a million runes.

I was not your ceremonial fuck, you are not the lost descendant of French settlers. At best, you are Canadian.

Afterward, you will say to the common friend: She is just saying that now. I heard her enjoy herself.

Was I wanting it? I wanted you to see. I am not that brown-haired girl. I was never the black-haired girl that I am. I was always the brown-haired girl, except with black hair.

A rock is a winged boy fallen to earth. If I let this go, then? How long does an indentation last, then? Your name is a narrowing lake in a chain of lakes. How can everything not be an echo of what was found and lost? Of the things we understood, when we stood at the shore collecting things? And still, we got lost.

It was a reunion. Their breasts bobbing like markers in Utowana. The tops of their breasts shimmering. The girl wanted to look nice. I was that girl. I am not that girl. Of the four Indians and one Sri Lankan in our class, only two of us returned. I should have worn what I always wore. Possibly ugly things. Loose things. Things that obscure. It is dangerous to be seen. It is stupid to think I could erase you.

A list of losses: this is a general idea of how I am arranged.

Trilobites are rocks that have already been washed and decorated in the ceremonial way.

Out of my nervousness, I asked for help.

She surveyed the map of me.

The shoes were fringed with sequins, more expensive than anything I had ever bought.

All I remembered later was that my feet were cold.

I could not walk home.

Nothing I wore that night could hold enough heat.

I wore a sweater, too thin. It was the night after Thanksgiving.

My clavicle could not speak and my arms were bare, hair rising.

Too thin for Newcastle after Newcastle.

Nothing I was could hold enough.

Nothing I could hold was enough.

My brother's wife and my mother waxed my arms, together, laughing, in the pink bathroom I grew up in, against the mirror I grew up seeing my face in. Here are the strips to lay down against the arms, thin as bones, and here is the rip of the leaving. Of the pulling away. Leaving my arms thin as branches, brushed to perfection.

A girl is a tree stripped of bark.

A girl is a skeleton, rock, shell.

A girl is a boy who cannot forget.

A boy is a girl who has learned not to see.

You told me later what I kept repeating.

I was very cold. Cover me, wrap your arms around me, be my overly friendly acquaintance; be my good brother, my hand-drifting uncle. It was Thanksgiving, for heaven's sake. I was not looking for a quick fuck. I was looking for warmth. I was looking for another you; I was looking for you. I wanted the weight of you.

Everyone else has moved on. I am still sitting here drinking coffee, listening to the garbage trucks pull up, listening to the people walking by. It is hot the way it is always hot in the city. You know how the heat comes in two directions, rising from the pavement, hard from the sun. I wanted to look nice. I did not want to be that girl I was. I drank enough fermented wheat to push her away until I could barely keep my balance. I drank enough cold beer so that the cold wasn't cold right away, so that I couldn't push you away.

I am trying to say it, to step up to the plate and claim it.

A girl is a memory pressed into stone.

You went to your reunion and then to hers. You were with her, your hand on the small of her back when she drank too much. You told me that her dress was black and red and clingy. I was angry at you for describing her dress that way. I think that was one of the many times it became clear which way things would go, and had been going all along.

You always have a choice. Every day you have a choice about how you will live your life and what stories you will tell about the choices you made.

You had the gift, like many people I have known, of making the story you tell seem to be the only story there is. This is what you said: I just need more time. This is what I understood: I am not enough. This is what I understand now: *there is no more time.*

You are only a shell. Or perhaps you are an Apache word for metal. Or: you are a petroglyph. No one can give someone else a reason. I believe in excavation. You believe in burying. It is better to make these distinctions. It is one way that I temper my eagerness to believe that you might have chosen differently.

I forced you in the end to say what we both knew. I wanted to hear you say that you loved her. I wanted you to say to me: *I don't love you anymore. I thought I did. Go home.* Humiliate me. I wanted the final humiliation so that I would not hope, never hope. It is a terrible trait of mine, of not believing something until it is pushed into words, and of believing words long after they are useful. Words are only words after all.

I am a trilobite, a regeneration in clay, a one-way sign. You have only to say my name, and I will appear: a silly incarnation of a sixteen-year-old. I am your atavistic hope: a minor goddess with a gift for calling, for incarnating, again and again. I am your worst nightmare: a vegetarian who won't go down on you. What kind of hedonism is that?

I had no words to tell you what happened. I could barely tell myself. I just knew that it would not have happened if you were there, and I wanted you to know that. I kept waking you the last night you slept next to me; I was awake and I was suffering. I wanted you to be able to read my mind, to comfort me. KNOW THIS. The girl who practiced on bananas gave better blow jobs and you knew it. I was not that girl. You chose what you had to.

I stumbled from one side of the wooden bar in its faux-NYC-loft-warehouse-look to the other, wanting your hand on the small of my back. Tonic. Your quiet laughter behind me. I would have been telling you about the kids in my elementary school classes, about who looked different, who looked better, and who looked worse.

I was saving up these stories to tell to you. Were you making a list in your head for someone else all this time? I made this into another reason to drink Newcastle.

Let me pretend you were with me all this time. I should have at least that. I would have walked you downstairs in my parents' house to the guest room bed and told you how to say, My name is ———, in Gujarati. *Maru nam———che.* I would have knocked into you and said, Tell me a story. You would have said, *V———, let me bring you back upstairs. You'll fall asleep downstairs. I don't want your parents mad. Come on, V———.*

After the last time you left, I sat down and cleaned my apartment. I opened the second file drawer, the lower one, the one I had never used, and began to sort out papers. I forced myself to look through files I had not looked at in years, to make decisions about what was still useful and what should be recycled to make room for the stacks of mail and paper I had accumulated in the time I had been thinking of you instead.

I returned to the bath, trying to enact intact. I wanted to return to intact.

A rock is a moon that has fallen to earth. Its concentric rings promise one side of the horizon to the other. Each rock, even the smooth ones, carry cracks.

Given sufficient heat, nearly any type of continental rock may melt. You barely fucked me. Granite rises, another form of regret. I think you barely loved me. Below a stone = the stillness of a flute. You were a mistake. Continents form through the process of accretion. I wanted you to see me. I want you to take it back. Erase you from between my ears. *Close your mouth, close your eyes and listen*: I was a mistake.

I tried to fit us together like a child takes the continents, pushes South America into Africa. You said, I'm no good for you. What looks like it should fit doesn't. I did not account for pulls. Fits and pulls are different forces altogether. I did not account for you and me. I did not account for getting stuck. Or the pills that I take every day to steady me, to keep not exalted and not below. I want to take it back.

Love is the name for a burial in what is now southern Utah.

Is that what love is, then, letting things lie?

Loss is a calling forth in middle Kentucky.

And my penchant for excavation? There is no name for this.

Love survives at 2:30 p.m. in middle Kentucky. These words will call forth.

We die for the smallest things. Nothing washes off—. I have died for the smallest things. Nothing washes off.

You left New York and returned to our colder town.

But what will I think about before I sleep?

Earlier brachiopods were called inarticulates.

Following the granite-forming period came a long period of erosion.

I am a suggestion, sunk into slate, beginning to harden.

A rock is a girl, rising from the earth—

companion texts

In *Living a Feminist Life,* queer theorist and scholar Sara Ahmed defines a companion text as "a text whose company enabled you to proceed on a path less trodden." These texts kept me company while I was making and remaking this book.

Margaret Atwood's "Nine Beginnings"
Sujata Bhatt's "Search for My Tongue"
adrienne maree brown's *Emergent Strategy: Shaping Change, Changing Worlds*
Kathleen Brogan's *Cultural Haunting: Ghosts and Ethnicity in Recent American Literature*
Theresa Hak Kyung Cha's *Dictee*
Victoria Chang's *Dear Memory: Letters on Writing, Silence, and Grief*
Gabrielle Civil's *the déjà vu: black dreams & black time*
Sheila Heti's *How Should a Person Be?*
bell hooks's *Talking Back: Thinking Feminist, Thinking Black*
Angela Jackson's "The Love of Travelers"
Bhanu Kapil's "Schizophrene"

Audre Lorde's *Sister Outsider: Essays and Speeches* and
   Zami: A New Spelling of My Name—A Biomythography
Carmen Maria Machado's *In the Dream House*
Deborah Miranda's *Bad Indians: A Tribal Memoir*
Toni Morrison's *Sula*
Jenny Odell's *How to Do Nothing: Resisting the Attention
   Economy*
Leah Lakshmi Piepzna-Samarasinha's *Care Work:
   Dreaming Disability Justice*
Claudia Rankine's *Don't Let Me Be Lonely, Citizen:
   An American Lyric,* and *Just Us: An American
   Conversation*
Adrienne Rich's *The Fact of a Doorframe*
Patrick Rosal's *Atang: An Altar for Listening to the
   Beginning of the World*
Reetika Vazirani's "It's a Young Country"
Alice Wong's *Year of the Tiger: An Activist's Life*

ephemera archive

1. Childhood Drawing (Courtesy of the author.)
2. Flower Basket (Courtesy of the author.)
3. Dance Notation (Reproduced with permission of Rathna Kumar.)
4. Workshop Letter (By Jim Foley, 2000. Reproduced with permission of Diane Foley.)
5. Snow Triptych (Courtesy of the author.)
6. Sonnet / Workshop Annotation (By Agha Shahid Ali, 1997. Reproduced with permission of Iqbal Ali.)
7. Ship, Port of Mombasa (By Natverlal Ambalal Shah, 1949. Courtesy of the author.)
8. Dance Notation Detail (Reproduced with permission of Rathna Kumar.)
9. Ship, Port of Mombasa, Double (By Natverlal Ambalal Shah, 1949. Courtesy of the author.)
10. Garland, En Route (Courtesy of the author.)
11. Autograph Book (Courtesy of the author.)
12. Workshop Letter (By Jim Foley, 2000. Reproduced with permission of Diane Foley.)

13. Major & Minor Keys (Courtesy of the author.)
14. *Aloha, Mother*, 1979 (Reproduced with permission of Joan Weetman.)
15. Jim Notebook (Photo of James Foley, transferred as a stamp onto a notebook cover, 2012. Image of James Foley reproduced with permission of Alice Martins. Notebook courtesy of Thomas Durkin. Photograph of the notebook by the author.)
16. Album Cover (B-Side / Loitering / Album Cover Northampton, 2001. Reproduced with permission of Greg Tulonen.)
17. Charcoal Collage (Courtesy of the author.)
18. Cobb's Hill / Pinnacle Hill (By Charles C. Zoller, 1917. Color transparency [autochrome]. Courtesy of the George Eastman Museum.)
19. Wooden Fence (Courtesy of the author.)

liner notes

The images in this book are artifacts, often personal, but they are not illustrations.

In the epigraph, Audre Lorde's words are excerpted from "An Interview: Audre Lorde and Adrienne Rich" in *Sister Outsider: Essays and Speeches* (Berkeley: Crossing Press, 2007), 83.

"Independence, Iowa" was performed at Luther College in Iowa in 2008 as part of the Black Earth Collaborative Arts Summer Coalescence presentation, "Ball's Out: Play to Win"; a site-specific performance of text, movement, and music exploring play and power. Grateful thanks to Jane Hawley, director of Black Earth Collaborative Arts, for inviting me to collaborate in generating and refining text and in performing. My heartfelt thanks to Sandhya and Brian Caton for hosting me in Iowa and to Marymount Manhattan College for funding my travel.

"Ithaca Is Never Far" is a retelling of *The Odyssey* from Penelope's point of view.

"The Granite State" was written in response to a call for writing to be included in *Ghazals for Foley: A Collection of Ghazals and Ghazal-Like Poetry* (HINCHAS Press), published and edited by Yago S. Cura in 2015 to honor American journalist James W. Foley. In the introduction to his anthology *Ravishing Disunities: Real Ghazals in English*, my teacher, poet and critic Agha Shahid Ali, wrote, "the ghazal goes back to seventh-century Arabia, perhaps even earlier, and its descendants are found not only in Arabic but in . . . Farsi, German, Hebrew, Hindi, Pashto, Spanish, Turkish, Urdu–and English . . . One definition of the word *ghazal*: It is the cry of the gazelle when it is cornered in a hunt and knows it will die." (Wesleyan University Press, 2000).

"Skeleton, Rock, Shell": "The excerpted text at the beginning of this story is taken from *Essentials of Earth History: An Introduction to Historical Geology,* from the chapter titled "The Invertebrates." I found this book at Blue Mountain Center, a place of magic which allowed me to conjure, hear, and write this story. "I have died for the smallest things. / Nothing washes off" are the final lines of "The Love of Travelers" by Angela Jackson, in *Callaloo: A Journal of African Diaspora Arts and Letters* (No. 35, Spring 1988).

"The Girl with Two Brothers" is for Sarah

"Divination" is for Phil

"Climate, Man, Vegetation" is for LeeAnne

"Watch Over Me; Turn a Blind Eye" is for Nathalal Dada

"The Half King" is for RNS

gratitudes & ghost tracks

Thank goodness for spirit, friendship, dance, creativity, and nature! And thank goodness for editors. I wish to thank the editors of the journals and anthologies in which some of these words first appeared: Mimi Khúc (*The Asian American Literary Review*); Purvi Shah, (*Asian Pacific American Journal*); Bradford Morrow (*Conjunctions*); Andrea Rexilius & Julia Cohen (*Denver Quarterly*); Ravi Shankar (*Drunken Boat*); Alisa Malinovich (*Generosity: a chapbook to benefit the Brooklyn Zen Center*); Yago S. Cura (*Ghazals for Foley*); Danit Brown (*Indiana Review*); Neelanjana Banerjee, Summi Kaipa, & Pireeni Sundaralingam (*Indivisible: An Anthology of Contemporary South Asian American Poetry*); Minna Zallman Proctor (*The Literary Review*); Kum-Kum Bhavnani (*meridians: feminism, race, transnationalism*); and Susan Steinberg (*Pleiades*). My thanks also to those publications in which reprints appeared: *Aster(ix)*; *Future Library: Contemporary Indian Writing*; *Indivisible*; and *Redux*. A special thanks to Kum-Kum, Brad, Minna, as well as Molly Sutton Kiefer for getting your hands in the weeds with me and for your attention to my words.

I am grateful to the following organizations for fellowships, residencies, or other support: the Anderson Center at Tower View; Blue Mountain Center; the Disability Visibility Project; the Kenyon Review Writers' Workshop for two Peter Taylor Fellowships; Kundiman—heart and community; Millay Arts; the New York Foundation for the Arts and the New York State Council for the Arts for a 2018 Fellowship in fiction; the Ragdale Foundation; the Constance Saltonstall Foundation; the Virginia Center for the Creative Arts for a 2019 George Edwards and Rachel Hadas Fellowship. I am especially grateful to BMC, Kundiman, and the New York Foundation for the Arts, which kept me going at times I had lost faith.

This book grew out of friendships, conversations, collaboration, and study with artists, dancers, teachers, students, and friends across *many* years and places. It's been over twenty years of creative encounters so any list I make is incomplete: a thousand threads go into the weaving. I know as soon as I send this, I will think of a dozen others who helped in the making of this book. However, in the final stretch, I relied on a few people in particular: I wish to especially thank my incredible assistant Abbey Frederick for her time and thoughtful engagement with this project and for wrangling these images; my dear friend Holly Wren Spaulding for reading this manuscript at its earliest stages; and Lorraine Bohonos, artist and wizard, for helping me manage ephemera, archives, and a move.

In the earliest days of these stories, Greg Tulonen—stalwart companion through the bramble. In later days: Sarah Adams, Neema Avashia, Katie Booth, Wendy Call, Erica Cavanagh, Gabrielle Civil, Natasha Chang, Karina Corrigan, Elena Creef, Tom Durkin, Jess Fenn, Katie Freeman, Ann Gagliardi, Nadia Ghent, Clare Morgana Gillis, Nina Ha, Emily Heaphy, Jennifer Ho, Madhu H. Kaza, Geeta Kothari, Uttara Bharath Kumar, Alessandra Leri, Magda Maczynska, Pat Malone, Ravi Mangla, Dawn Lundy Martin, Nora Maynard, Suketu Mehta, Deborah Miranda, Nick Montemarano, Sara Nolan, Deesha Philyaw, Ann Poduri, Leslie Roberts, Melissa Sandor, Margie Searl, Kyle Semmel, Monica Shah, Sue Stein, Megan Stielstra, Renee Simms, Rajesh Singaravelu, Ren vanMeenen, Dena B. Vardaxis, Andrew Varnon, Stephen West, Alice Wong, and Mary Kay Zuravleff. This list is not exhaustive: if you think you belong here, you do. I could not have gotten through this process without friends and fellow artists.

As always, thanks to my teachers: the good, the not-so-good, the definitively bad, and the all-time greats. I learned from all of you.

For reading this and other versions of this manuscript over the years, I thank Steve Woodward. For sensitivity reads on "The Girl with Two Brothers" and "The Half King," I wish to thank Gretchen Potter and Angelique Stevens. For their art historian and artist eyes on the ephemera archive, I thank Sarah Adams and Georgia Wall.

We don't do it alone. I am grateful to the community I found within HIVE, JOI hiking, SWeNJ, TBK Collective, Friday Feminist Co-working, and WMC's #LKRP. Also: I thank all the friends I've walked and talked with, especially during the pandemic.

My artistic process of writing and revising includes improvisational somatic movement forms such as contemplative dance/authentic movement, 5Rhythms, and other ecstatic dance; sonic imaging—repetition of songs/tracks/chanting/mystic/music trance; sifting through my personal archives and classifying ephemera and rocks; and enacting rituals and shrine/altar building. Ultimately, I realized that this work, this book, these stories are a kind of elegy. And these shrines, these cairns, and poems as rock-building, built the book.

Thank you to all the folks on Instagram who interacted with the dances I posted during a lonely and grief-filled early pandemic and quarantine. You helped me realize there was something communicated through movement that connected to the work of making this book. Thank you to my dance teachers, especially Dorothy Hershkowitz, Lucia Horan, Daphne Lowell, and Rathna Kumar. It has been incredible to study with so many of you again via Zoom. Thanks to PJ Pennewell, Cat Willis, and Natalie Rogers-Cropper for conversations about discipline, practice, movement, and freedom. Thank you to Cat for that first dance on IG, which also made me want to share dance beyond performance.

Thank you to Garth Fagan Dance for the aesthetic: the creation of a technique combining African traditions and Caribbean stories to expand the world of American modern dance inspired me as a writer with roots in East Africa and South Asia to make my own way. In Gujarati (and Hindi/Urdu), the word for yesterday and tomorrow is the same: kaal/kaaleh. Its meaning is distinguished by context. Kaaleh simultaneously holds both past and future and these stories do the same—time is not linear in these cultures; rather, time is circular and elliptical, moves in fits and starts and expands multi-dimensionally.

Writing is something I've always done. Publishing and preparing a book for publication is a whole other thing. As a disabled writer with manic depression and ADHD, I was able to make this book because I had access to healthcare, health insurance, acupuncture, medication, and other modalities. I am grateful to those who helped me manage my health: my primary care doctor, Dr. Andrea Ferrantino; my psychiatrist, Dr. Catherine Flannery; Bev Gold, Emery Jones, Courtney Robertson, and Barbara Russell. Finishing a project is hard. Thanks to all those who held space for me in a midwifery way, especially Cath Hopkins—crip doula and compassionate friend—Wendy, Geeta, Gabrielle, Magda, Marjana, Holly, Kate, Katie, and Kitty. Rahul, for all the flower compositions and kind questions, and Alice Wong for the cute stickers, wonderful cards, tiger warrior posts, and nineties movie recommendations.

Thank you to my agent, Sarah Burnes, who got these stories and said YES when I said I was thinking about images—right away and with great enthusiasm. I'm so grateful! Thank you to Sophie Pugh-Sellers for scheduling and following up. My thanks to everyone at West Virginia University Press, especially former director Derek Krissoff for reaching out to ask if I had a manuscript and being the number one reason you are holding this book in your hands; Sarah Munroe, editor and interim director, for her thoughtful questions, edits, and brilliant suggestion to move the soundtrack from where it was hidden in the back of the book; managing editor Sara Georgi for giving me such a clear road map; and Troy Wilderson, who copyedited this book with sensitivity and sharpness, in a collaborative way. Thank you also to Jeremy Wang-Iverson for getting the word out and to Than Saffel for making a beautiful cover. A special thanks to those who wrote reader reports, especially Rahul Mehta and Jon Pineda. You helped me make this book better. Finally, I am grateful to Deesha Philyaw and Lidia Yuknavitch for their fierce words.

Thanks to my family—especially to my parents for their prayers, belief in me, and all the food and cooking; my brother for being my brother, and to Raj for steering the craft in stormy weather. My dad was a serious reader, admirer of writers, and wanted to know why the book was taking this long to be published, because hadn't I had already written it?! I'm sorry you didn't get to see the cover, Dad, but glad you weighed in on the title.

While working on this book, I mourned the passing of my uncle, Kirit N. Shah, a writer and poet who also loved to dance, on February 12, 2021. Exactly one year later, on February 12, 2022, my friend and former editor Valerie Boyd died. She was the mentor I hadn't known I was looking for. That spring Urvashi Vaid, a civil rights and gay and lesbian rights activist and advocate whose life affected my generation and beyond, also passed, far too young. This book is dedicated in part to them and the way they made room for other voices. I also thank Jim Foley and LeeAnne Smith White. These stories are for the friends of my youth, which will always include you.

Jim, James Wright Foley, was a talented fiction writer and my graduate school classmate during the years of 1999–2002. His "Notes to a Fellow Educator," a short story about a teacher named James Foley, won the prestigious *Indiana Review* fiction prize in 2001. His presence and friendship made any classroom or party better and an unsafe workshop situation more bearable. Jim later became a freelance text reporter and video journalist. He found his voice telling other people's stories. In 2014, Jim was the first American hostage murdered by ISIS in Syria. His family later established the James W. Foley Legacy Foundation to promote journalist safety and to advocate for the return of American hostages. To learn more about Jim, please visit https://jamesfoley-foundation.org.

Rana Zoe Mungin is a Black Afro-Latina writer, a teacher, a Brooklynite and a fellow alumna of Wellesley College. Zoe died at age thirty of COVID-19 after having been turned away from hospitals and refused treatment *twice*. Journalist Karen Grigsby Bates noted that Mungin's graduate degree was awarded from a program where she received a fellowship and stipend, but that they "came at a considerable cost" (*Wellesley* Magazine, Fall 2020). In 2015, Mungin said, "There is a marked lack of safety in being a woman of color dedicated to creating art in white spaces. The time I spent completing my MFA was a period of physical, sexual, and emotional danger, which isn't indicative of how someone else's experience may go; this is just what happened to me" (Wellesley Underground).

I attended the same program, many years before Zoe. It is *never* just one person. There are always many stories, but not all stories get through—not all stories are heard, listened to, or believed. We have to keep speaking. We have to keep walking. Many voices form a chorus— stories light a path through the hills and forest.

greg tulonen

&

sejal shah

"The door itself / makes no promises. It is only a door." ~adrienne rich

live lit atticus books 7:30 p.m. friday 3/30/01